About the Author

Tom Mutch is an Australian who lives on the Coromandel Peninsula of New Zealand. He is an artist who works in many mediums from painting to film-making. He also loves to write. He is married with three grown-up children.

We loved having you stay with us at Coromandel Views Bed + Breakfast.

From Nicola + Graeme.

Superbird

The Truth Stream

The third and final Superbird novel by
Tom Mutch

LIM PUBLISHING

Copyright © Tom Mutch, 2007

Published 2007 by Lim Publishing,
Birds Nest Studio, Kuaotunu, RD2, Whitianga, New Zealand
www.tommutch.com

Distributed by David Bateman Ltd
30 Tarndale Grove, Albany, Auckland, New Zealand

ISBN 978-1-86953-707-4

This book is copyright. Except for the purpose of fair review, no part may be stored or transmitted in any form or by any means, electronic or mechanical, including recording or storage in any information retrieval systems, without permission in writing from the publisher. No reproduction may be made, whether by photocopying or by any other means, unless a licence has been obtained from the publisher or its agent.

Cover: oil paintings by Tom Mutch
Front cover: *Superbird and Mt Cloudcatcher*, 2005
Back cover: *Keywee in the Truth Stream*, 2001
Cover design: Jag Design Ltd, Auckland
Typesetting: Purrfect Grafix Ltd, Auckland
Printed in China through Colorcraft Ltd, Hong Kong

Acknowledgements

for Rachel Emile Ben Amelia

Dream if you like about a place
A new hope for the human race
We've spent it all
There's not much left
Clean waters gone
The air's a mess
And traffic noise and buildings spread
Birds disappear,
There's no shell fish
Cry if you like, there's not enough
Money in the bank makes me really laugh
I looked up to you
Hoped that you could pull us through
I realise, no surprise
You were just looking after you
(from the song titled *Afterlife* © Mutch, 1990)

This is the final book in the trilogy *The Truth Stream*
The first being *The Birth of Superbird*
followed by *In an Upside Down World*.

I hope you enjoyed the journey.
A very warm thanks to you all. Peace and Prosperity.
Tom Mutch, 2007

Preface

Book One ~ *The Birth of Superbird*
The Birth of Superbird, told of the daring escape from Lair City of the Half-light Solo, his friends, the human children Bella and Race, and his beloved dog Ubu.

That story culminated in the birth of the mythical Epic of the Superbird Race, son of the mystic Sansvira, and the defeat of the evil Zekai Manci's creature Smelt, who had been sent to hunt down the refugees.

Book Two ~ *In an Upside Down World*
Part 1 delivers the shocking events that have led to Lair City's birth, and the history of the Undercity and Shanks's Dynasty. Here we find the Truth Stream fighting back, and the power that resides in the boughs of Oak, 'The-Tree-That-Never-Sleeps'.

Part 2 sees Epic, Solo and Ubu, accompanied by Neke the mystical snake and Nua of the Kuaha, return to Lair City.

Book Three ~ *The Truth Stream*
The Truth Stream opens with the retreat of those that have survived the battle for Lair City, escaping across the Great River.

Zekai Manci's rule is over. Epic, Solo and Nua struggle to centre themselves, to understand their place within the complexity of the Truth Stream, isolating themselves from the Kuaha village, only to return stronger, in readiness for the final conflict with the Aliens.

Woven through this fast-paced saga of conflict is a delightful twist; an imaginative leap that delivers a new dimension to the trilogy. A marvellous fantasy that lifts one's spirit.

Chapter One

The Mancirian craft arrived, slicing apart the permanent smog, the miasma that hung over Lair City. It landed, wedging itself between the high-rises, shattering windows, sending shards of deadly glass ripping through the air. The ship's after-burners melted the Rim rails and pools of molten steel bubbled, spitting toxic fumes into the insipid light. A bellowing inferno leapt from the ship's undercarriage as it settled with a groan, upright, disappearing inside its own cloud of gas and vapours.

Buildings swayed, toppling masonry that flipped, bouncing off the metallic monster's sides. Huge slabs dropped like bombs, exploding on impact and sending shrapnel flying around the heads of the fleeing inhabitants. The noise was horrific, intolerable. Humans clutched their ears, crumpled, squirming into foetal positions among the debris that rained down from above, squashing Lairs and people alike. With a final rumble, and a satisfied hiss that echoed into the Undercity and across the Great River, the spaceship cut its engines.

The sticky yellow mist of Lair City curdled a blood-chilling red, illuminating the carnage and the retreating survivors of the frantic battle that had been taking place.

The Library steps were strewn with corpses that, for the briefest moment, seemed to jump back to life in the infra-red flash. The illusion was soon put to rest as a myriad lights, beamed from the craft, flooded the quadrangle. A portal opened, projecting a causeway to anchor the humming machine that filled the giant square within the monolithic structures of the city.

A black, indistinguishable mass wobbled its way out of the gaping doorway and down the ramp, escorted by spindly forms clutching containers with tubes that were locked to all parts of the jelly-like creature. The forms inched their way out from under the ship's shadow to take their first steps into the searing light. Detached from the madness combusting around them, they watched Lairs hunting down Undercity humans – those that were still alive. They were being mercilessly tracked, cornered and torn apart in the labyrinths the Lairs knew all too well. Those humans lucky enough still to be in the control room were left with no choice but to ride the elevator back down to Level One, to dwell underground once again.

'It's a primitive world you have created for your kind, Zebu. You Mancirians are fortunate to have collaborated with us Jaars. Soon you will have no need for your container; you will be free of your tubes and hosing, and able to walk the city in an atmosphere that we alone have the power to manipulate. Lairs will be surplus to your needs. How antiquated they are – clumsy and unpredictable. They are neither human nor machine; outdated engineering. It's irritating to watch their careless handling of the dead. Jaars would keep them in one piece. The odour is unpleasant, an insult to my nose. So many bodies, what will you do with them?'

'You leave that to us, Laxman. The Lairs will dispose of them. What is it to you?'

'They could be used to feed our Master-tree.'

'You can have some, though we have our own uses for them, as you know. How long will it take your Jaars to convert my city? I'm not looking forward to inhabiting Zekai's dome.'

Laxman leaned into the Mancirian, his spindly body bending with ease. 'Not long, Zebu, not long at all. And what will become of Zekai Manci?' Laxman asked.

'He will be transported back to Manci. His life there will be horrid.'

* * * * * * *

Zekai's dome closed in on him. The tubes and hosing that fed his translucent jelly frame now wrapped his body as a spider's web wraps its prey. The tip of his foot-long tongue licked at the inside of his lips across his needle-sharp teeth. His breathing came in little sharp gulps like a goldfish mouthing the surface of a pond. Zekai's monitors fizzed, the screen a speckled mass of white creating the impression his city was being attacked by a snowstorm.

He was waiting; waiting for his Superior to transport him back to his own planet, to a life with no future, never to mate, to live outside his own society. A failure, an untouchable, a leper. He would be castigated, belittled in front of his own. He'd seen it happen to others.

What was to have been the start of a glittering career, the first of many planets he'd hoped to control, was now just a jagged lump in his constricting throat. Zekai lifted his massive talons, and flaying wildly, ripped the tubes and hosing from his body. His head lit up like neon as parts shook loose inside his bulbous, transparent head. His body turned as black as coal dust and violent spasms racked him. A putrid concoction spewed from his mouth, spilling, collecting in his lap where his gross tongue now trembled. He let out a rattling cry as he slumped forward, his talons twitching, to dangle over the edge of his chair.

* * * * * * *

A fierce wind whipped at the heels of those fleeing Lair City. The Lairlights, burdened with dead Kuaha warriors slung over their shoulders, struggled to keep pace. Otahi, Nua and Solo brought up the rear, urging them all forward.

The humans from the Undercity needed no coaxing, jumping over Lairs freshly slaughtered by Otahi's point men. They sprinted for the bridge, where the waters of the Great River were in upheaval.

A terrifying torrent of dervish whirlpools surged around the bridge. Whitecaps crashed erratically against the pylons pelting spray and foam across the creaking timbers that swayed and jerked, making the crossing as difficult as balancing on the deck of a small boat tossed around at sea.

The Lairlights had to be steadied, propped by the hands of the grieving warriors who were petrified of losing one of their dead to the waves that snatched at the unstable bridge.

Bringing up the rear, Jall was the last to cross, the only one to hold his nerve, with legs planted wide, his body tipping from side to side, riding the structure's movement. He had his hands thrust deep into his Greatcoat pockets fingering Oak's acorns, his eyes searching, looking for stragglers and watching for Rim lights.

Satisfied he was alone, Jall spun around, momentarily hanging in the air, arms spreadeagled, as his massive hands clutching the acorns hurled the seeds into the raging river. His body fell to the bridge. He rolled on impact, was back on his feet and onto dry land.

Solo and Nua stood close together. Their pinched, dejected faces followed Jall's progress as he strode towards them on the ridge. Solo slumped to the ground, grinding his teeth, despair replacing his anger as he watched a line of Lairs seal off the bridge.

Nua placed his hand on Solo's head, then turned to join Otahi and the other Kuaha warriors who, glad of his company, were gathered in a tight group tending to their wounds and covering the dead with ponga fronds.

Those humans – a shabby bunch – who had managed to escape the Undercity eyed the Lairlights with suspicion, their mutterings festering into outright contempt and hatred for the half-converted Lairs. 'Send them back to their own,' one bellowed. 'They can't be trusted.'

'How do we know they won't throttle us in our sleep?' another yelled.

'Yes, yes, I'm with you. Let's finish them. Who wants to look at their evil screens a moment longer?'

The jittery Lairlights, screens rolling, looping erratically, fingers twitching, moved from jackboot to jackboot, edging away from the aroused mob towards the Kuaha Warriors. The threatening words grabbed Solo's attention. He'd heard enough. He sprang to his feet as the Lairlights were circled by the very people they had helped to save. He rushed at the ring, sending bodies sprawling.

'You'll have to get past me first,' he screamed.

'Then we will,' a ginger-headed face yelled back, flinging a fist which sailed past Solo's nose. They pressed forward, their confidence building, only to retreat as Neke emerged from Solo's jacket, hissing and spitting. She hit the ground ready to strike. She flung herself around the feet of the retreating circle. Then the scuffle came to Nua's attention. He leaped across the clearing at the ginger-headed assailant and floored the foolish troublemaker with one mighty slap.

'Why have we bothered to save a stupid, ungrateful rabble like you lot? All of you. Go, stand under that tree,' he demanded, sending the now-silenced ginger-headed agitator scrambling away on all fours like a beaten dog towards the tree.

'Are you alright, Solo?' Nua asked, his lips twisting into a snarl, his eyes bulging in amazement as he glanced across the small clearing to see Jall loitering, arms folded over his chest with a queer smirk on his face.

'What are you smiling about?' Nua called. 'These are your own kind. Lairlights. And you stand by and do nothing. Are you a coward? Would you watch Solo be hurt protecting them and do nothing? There is rot in you. Something foul.'

'I'm not a Lairlight. I'm human. I was never converted as you know, and smile, yes, I was smiling because I knew you would handle it. I found it intriguing, nothing more. Besides, who would argue with Neke?'

'Nua, leave off. Jall has proved himself. It's the humans from the Undercity who need to be chastised. Look at them, huddled together like scared rabbits. All our efforts and losses for so few. They have never been in the Truth Stream. They have only known darkness and servitude. It will take time. They do not understand yet that they are free, that they are safe.'

'I tell you, Solo, something's not right with that one,' Nua insisted, gesturing with his club in Jall's direction.

'You are tired and emotional. You have suffered much this day. Please, we need to contemplate our situation, not argue and fight. Go bury your dead, and then your confusion will also be put to rest. There's little more we can do right now. Go and be with your chief. He needs you.'

Jall waited for Nua to depart, then strolled over to Solo and chuckled. 'He's wrong, you know. His problems are his own. You do agree, don't you?'

Solo looked hard into Jall's eyes. His strong, square face stared unflinchingly back, perfect in its flexibility, its human proportions. He reached up to pat Solo's shoulder, confidence oozing from his every move.

'Nua is a proud warrior and he can be volatile. It would help if you mingled with the Lairlights more often,' Solo suggested.

'Of course, I will go and join them. They look a little timid. They are lucky that you and Nua have their safety at heart.'

'Jall, keep them separated from the people of the Undercity. In time they will accept the Lairlights' plight and understand they are human too.'

They made two separate camps that night, the humans bickering away in their own little corner of the woods, the Kuaha at the opposite side of the clearing. The Lairlights, screens glowing dully under the canopy of fir, moved closer to the Kuaha who sat around a small fire. Jall sat next to Chief Otahi.

'Forgive Nua's outburst. He can be hot-headed,' Otahi whispered into Jall's ear. 'He will cool down; his bond with Solo is brotherly. Nua,' Otahi called through the smoke, 'come sit with us. Let us discuss the future of the Undercity humans and that of the Lairlights.'

Nua, who had deliberately kept his distance from Jall, heaved himself upright, expelling a disgruntled lung-full of air into the still night, unmistakable in its displeasure. He had no choice but to do his Chief's bidding.

Tapping the ground, Otahi said, 'Sit. Tell me your thoughts. Jall has told me of his admiration for your battle skills. He speaks highly of your courage. He wishes you would trust him.'

Nua grunted, scoffing at rather than acknowledging his chief's words. Jall, who had been looking at him over Otahi's shoulder, turned his head and spat into the dark.

'Solo has counted the Undercity folk,' Otahi said. 'There are seventeen. I have decided to take them back to our village. They can live on the borders of our lands. Hopefully they will live in harmony with the Lairlights. Solo has reminded me that he will find a formula from Oak's seed and release the Lairlights from their caged state. They will return to their human selves. Just like Jall here.' He put his arm around Jall.

This was too much for Nua. 'Well,' he said, 'you don't need my help to discuss anything here,' and he pushed himself upright. With downcast eyes, he catapulted away, walking out into the trees glad of his own company and that of the owl which hooted overhead.

Still smarting from the ungrateful antics of the humans, Solo lumbered across to the huddled group. 'You are now dependent on the Kuaha and the Lairlights for your welfare,' he said. 'If you cannot live with this, you will be forced back down the ridge into the fingers of the Lairs. What's your name?' Solo demanded, grabbing the ginger-headed bloke who was nursing his swollen, bruised cheek.

'Cullum,' he replied meekly.

'Shall we send you down first, Cullum?' Solo asked, releasing his grip. Cullum backed away.

'No, I thought not. Make up your minds. You have until daybreak.'

Solo set off to look for Nua. He found his friend looking miserable, wrapped inside his tattered cloak and clearly struggling with his own thoughts, the missing feathers like symbols of his state of mind.

'I know it's illogical Solo. After all, Oak and Superbird have promoted Jall, yet I cannot shake off this feeling I have. I know Jall is not true of heart.'

'But Nua, how could Jall deceive Oak and Epic? That would be impossible. Surely. And look at your brother Chief Otahi. He too enjoys Jall's company.'

'My mana is stripped in front of my people when he sucks up to Otahi, my own brother. I want so much to smash the grin from his face with my club. When he told us that Oak would be burnt to the ground, it was as if he enjoyed his vile prediction.'

'Nua, he spoke on Oak's behalf. You know that. Just keep away from Jall.'

'Well, Solo, what are your feelings about the Halflight?'

'I have no reason to doubt Jall. He is not my favourite company, yet I hold no grudge.'

'Grudge! Grudge! Is that how you see it? Leave me. I want to be alone. Go! I thought you, of all people, would understand.'

Nua pulled his cloak tight around his body, dismissing Solo.

Solo walked away, his gaze following his feet, each step lost in the turmoil of his fatigued mind. He found a place between the roots of a puriri tree and dozed fitfully, troubled by Nua's stubbornness. The swaying branches of the puriri rubbed together overhead, competing with his tormented thoughts, chanting the sound of Nua's name.

The morning brought a more settled camp; a delegation from the Undercity apologised to the Lairlights and Nua at Otahi's side.

Solo, bleary-eyed and grumpy from lack of sleep, and yet to lock his brain into gear, just nodded as he passed. A wry smile creased his lips when he remembered Neke cursing into the night as she flung herself from his pocket to find a safe place to slumber, afraid of being flattened by his fitful movements.

He dragged his aching body across the clearing to the ridgeline, swinging his arms about to aid circulation. His limbs were stiff and sore, and he was still trying to piece together his struggle to make sense of Nua's attitude towards Jall. He placed the knuckles of his index fingers in his gummed eyes, erasing the sleep that stuck to his eyelids. He rubbed with more vigour, blinking, unable to trust his vision, stunned by what he saw. 'Nua,' he yelled, 'come look at this!'

The excitement in his voice attracted the entire camp. Below them, the Truth Stream bridge had been obliterated, washed away. Lairs were still mincing around on the opposite bank. The dreaded city was mothballed in its own disgusting smog.

Otahi gathered them all around him. 'The village of the Kuaha is two days' march from here. It is to there we will go. We will rebuild, strengthen ourselves. The Ahorangi will bless our homecoming. You will learn the ways of the Kuaha. In time, we will take back all that is ours. I now know that this is our destiny. I have seen with my own eyes the evil that is Lair City. We will return wiser.'

'Yes, wisdom is a great gift, Chief Otahi,' a voice proclaimed from overhead. 'It can take many forms and is hard to hold.'

The group erupted into rapturous applause as Epic's life force materialised next to the Chief. 'I bring news of our foes and the state of Lair City. News that will be hard to swallow, information that will test your wisest. But first, Solo must collect Oak's acorns from the Halflights. They are the treasure of all treasures. So give them to him for safe-keeping and our future. Come, empty your pockets, let us see Oak's seeds. Place them here in front of us all.'

The Lairlights stepped forward, proud to be carriers of such prestigious cargo. They formed a single line in front of Solo, each one pulling two gloved handfuls of the acorns from his pockets. Their screens glowed a delicate yellow, then cleared to expose their true identities, their human selves, their captive faces pleading to be released from their macabre boxes. As they placed the acorns at his feet, Solo embraced each one, promising that he would spare nothing in his effort to make them human again.

The Undercity folk, gob-smacked at seeing human faces inside the Lairlight's screens, let out cries of astonishment.

'And yours, Jall,' Nua asked, 'where are they?'

'I have none. They were lost when I fell crossing the bridge. They spilled from my coat. They were swept away into the Great River.'

Nua's heart skipped a beat. He clenched his fists into a ball at his side. There was an uneasy silence, broken by the call of a bellbird, the imitator of the tui, endorsing Jall's charade in Nua's mind.

'I tried desperately to save them. It all happened so quickly, I had no choice but to save myself.'

Nua's eyes flashed like a bolt of lightning, striking Solo's. His face had the look of a man whose words had been proved just. Solo found it impossible to hold Nua's glare, his thoughts tumbling back into the black hole of the previous night. He kicked at a branch tangled in the grass at his feet.

* * * * * * *

'Let's settle you into your dome,' Laxman said to Zebu as they threaded their way though the rubble towards the control room entrance. Lairs were busy dragging the dead that littered the corridor into the chaotic streets. The two aliens had to wait, perched on a slab of metal among the lifeless corpses. Mangled human and Lair limbs intertwined in growing heaps. Zebu sucked hard on the container percolating by his feet.

'Soon you will be able to walk the city in an atmosphere suited to our needs,' Laxman suggested. 'The Master-tree is being brought forth as we speak. It will take control as soon as its roots claim the earth. Then its offspring will run and sprout. Its saplings will populate the streets. They will purify this pollution into the carbon dioxide that makes for healthy life. The Lairs will need converters or they will perish before we can re-supply the work force from below. Your Undercity stocks are well preserved, I take it?'

'Where will you place the Master-tree?' Zebu asked, ignoring Laxman's question.

'Acheron Afrit will choose for itself. The Master-tree is the centre of the universe. All Jaars know this. Its intelligence is beyond our comprehension. The tree of life has always been with us. It is Creation itself. We worship its roots, limbs and spikes and in return it gives life itself. Acheron Afrit is timeless. Before time. The Master-tree is infinite and knows our every thought. The tree of life knows our every action. Acheron Afrit is all-powerful. We Jaars feel it is a defect in Mancirian genes that you need animal products for your nourishment. Perhaps you will evolve to be like us, dependent only on the carbon dioxide we breathe. In this, we find all the goodness that one requires. We are the chosen. The Master-tree has blessed us. You should pray that it also blesses you.'

'Without us Mancirians, you could not colonise this planet. Jaars need us to break it open through our technology and might. Don't rant to me about your superior evolution. Jaars are parasites that come to pick over the worlds we conquer.'

Laxman's eyelids twitched. His sooty yellow, cat-like pupils flicked, magnified by the scrolling watery shields that indicated his displeasure at Zebu's words. The tight-fitting lycra material that covered his skin rippled as he flexed his bony fingers. He opened his mouth wide and bared his blunt grey teeth as if to take a bite out of Zebu's jelly frame, then shut it, clamping down on his gums – a typical Jaar reaction when agitated.

Zebu struggled to his feet, his taloned hands holding the tubes that connected to his container. 'Well,' he said, 'are you going to help?'

The Jaar bent over like a willow and lifted the container from the pavement, clearly not happy to be following the Mancirian as he staggered down the corridor to the elevator in the empty control room.

Laxman pressed a button. The lift doors opened and shut with a *whoosh*. They arrived at Zekai's dome. Laxman unplugged Zebu, who drifted out into the airless space expecting to find Zekai pleading for redemption. Instead Zebu found him dangling, wrapped in his own web of tubes, fluids dripping from his extended tongue, dead. He uncoupled Zekai and towed him back to the elevator to stuff the decomposing blob into the lift, jamming Laxman into the corner.

'Wait, I need to find Zekai's tag. It has his service record, numbers, imprinted within its metal disc. It's not on his body. Most unusual. He would need it to return to Manci. Without it, he would be seen as a drone or even an impostor. Not that it matters much to him now. I can't find it. It's not here,' Zebu said, returning to the lift.

'Zekai will still have to be returned to Manci,' he went on, somewhat out of breath. 'Have him covered before you take him through the streets to our craft. It would do neither of us any good for him to be seen by the Lairs.'

'I'll get my Jaars to take care of it,' Laxman said, his skinny fingers pinching at his flat nose, pleased that he had the protection of his own biosphere. Yes, he too would be grateful when the Master-tree found its place in Lair City and he no longer had to generate his own atmosphere.

* * * * * * *

A cry of anguish swept through the Undercity. The euphoria of freedom that had embraced the Levels suddenly turned to nightmarish screams. A retreating wave of humans crashed back into themselves as Lairs minced their way from the lift doors, cutting a swathe through the packed vault. Humans fell like cornstalks at harvest. Their primitive weapons were no match for the Lairs' dangerous fingers. It was a brief encounter, a desperate surge, a stampede, crushing those not sturdy enough to climb over each other. The pitiful shriek from one pinned, cut in half, was silenced by the iron door slamming shut.

* * * * * * *

Silk shivered, weeping, as she slipped down the wall that had been supporting her, collapsing into a ball. Her beautiful face was hidden by her matted hair that dropped to the grimy floor, her feet wrapped in the hem of her shift. Her mind battled with visions and knowledge that she had no right to own – flashes of Epic and Solo out in the Truth Stream, Neke wound around Solo's arm, and of the grotesque deformed trunk and branches of Acheron Afrit, the Master-tree, being trolleyed through Lair City, its roots writhing, unfurling, striking out in search of its preferred ground.

It was the buffeting, the knocks to her body that brought Silk back. A rabid mob was laying claim to the better parts of Mt Paris, determined to step into the Shanks Dynasty shoes. Pillaging, quarrelsome souls, whose aggression laid waste to any notions of order and civil rights. Hell had returned to the Undercity.

Like a sleepwalker, Silk descended to her parents' apartment on the sixth level to find several bodies poisoned by the Orabanche's phlegm. She was amazed by the hideous creature's toxicity and guarded the door until she found help to drag the bodies and all the apartment's contents into the Great Hall where they would be burned. She then returned to the empty shell and crumpled into a corner, her heart stung by the meanness of human beings, isolated and besieged by a sickness that attacked her being. She meditated by counting the number of steps it would take to reach Mt Paris. To each step she gave a name: justice, liberty, faith, hope, forgiveness, truth, love, honesty. She fell into a stupor at last, a deadly malaise. Deprived of nourishment, her body shrivelled and her mind simply stopped.

The elders found her frail and half-frozen. They had her stretchered above to Mt Paris and with infinite care, retrieved her from her comatose state. It was a slow process and when she did recover, she became a recluse; silent and distant though watched over by the elders who gave her the space she needed.

'Give her time, Elder Watts.'

'But she needs to see how the Undercity has developed, blossomed. The people cry out for her. They know that she is the one; our Oracle, our direct line to Superbird and Neke. She will be amazed at the transformation that has taken place. We must get her to leave her dwellings, to see with her own eyes the miracle of a civilised Undercity.'

'I'm sure she can sense the energy,' Otis said, 'she will appear when she is ready.'

* * * * * * *

Laxman made his way out into the streets of Lair City. The Master-tree sat dormant on its trolley, covered by a clear plastic dome, its roots void of dirt, hibernating in its protective shell. Its smooth bark, a ghostly alabaster skin, displayed a multitude of veins that laced its trunk and disappeared into its gnarly, contorted leafless branches.

Laxman clasped his hands together and purred. The greatest wonder in the Galaxy was about to be released. He let out a contented sigh. The Master-tree, surrounded by Jaars, was a magnificent sight that sent a thrilling chill up his spine. A hush hung in the floodlights glaring from the ship. Lairs lined the streets in awe. Their screens just ticking over, they moved trance-like from side to side, swaying, their fingers stretching and retracting. Laxman smiled to himself and looked directly into a camera. He knew Zebu would be glued to the monitors in his dome, suspiciously watching his every move. He raised his hand to acknowledge the Mancirian, then pointed to the Lairs and grinned. Zebu, agitated, fidgety, squirmed in his chair. There was an uneasy silence in the city. The normal hum of Rim on rail could not be heard, the streets devoid of normal clatter, and the air ripe with expectation, as if the city was holding its breath. Laxman savoured the moment.

'Release Acheron Afrit, the all-knowing one,' he hollered. The Jaars jumped to his command and peeled back the covering. Instantly, the Master-tree's roots quivered and its branches clicked together, tapping out a pulpy rhythm, groping, twisting, feeling for themselves. Springing out, splayed in all directions, while it jacked itself up by its frantic roots that had slipped down the sides of the trolley, like an octopus, its tendrils anchored to the pavement. It heaved itself higher, breaking its bond to the carriage. In one co-ordinated effort, the Jaars streamed in to push the trolley clear, the timing precise, drilled into them by Laxman.

Laxman looked back at the camera and raised his fist to the lens.

Now, the Master-tree stood supporting itself, rigid, straining, creaking, stretching its boughs.

Then it happened. The tree exploded into movement, like a centipede, its roots carried it racing from one corner to the next, up this street, down another. It was impossible to know which way it would turn, trampling anything that blocked its path, its limbs smashing against buildings, its roots climbing over any obstacle, tearing at slabs of concrete, burrowing into cracks then backtracking to where it had started. Rubble flew, Lairs were flattened, rims flung into the air. The

Jaars sang out its name in chorus. 'Acheron Afrit, Acheron Afrit,' they chanted. Then it scrambled down Library Lane, leaving a trail of destruction in its wake.

Just as dramatically, it stopped in the middle of Data Street. The Jaars all screamed in unison. All protocol abandoned, they made their way towards the tree. Laxman was yelling out orders. 'Fill the trolley,' he cried, 'the Master-tree will be hungry.'

Data Street was brimming with Jaars. They ringed the tree, only giving way to the dead and dying that were being pushed up to the tree.

Now the Master-tree's roots went to work drilling into the street's surface, rearing up and crashing down, pulling the paving apart. It opened up a crater, its limbs chattering away, bouncing off each other in a berserk display of raw power. A cavity could be clearly seen at the base of its trunk. Its branches bent towards the trolley of cadavers, clamping vice-like, piercing the bodies, scooping them into the air, then jamming them into the mouth-like crevice. With each body, the Jaars screamed out the Master-tree's name. In this way, it devoured the entire offering from the carriage.

Now it settled its roots deep into the abyss below its trunk. Its bark, pulsating, flooded, already gorging on its grisly meal, turning the tree a dark crimson colour. Spikes and thorny leaves popped out from all parts of its boughs. The Jaars, delirious, ran to touch their marvel, placing their foreheads against its trunk, breathing in deep gulps of the carbon dioxide that the tree now exhaled.

****

Zebu Manci too, had a need to create his own monster. A Lair that would answer only to him. He flirted with the idea of programming a command, a word, that would activate the assassination of Laxman if required, but then he recanted; his own knowledge of alchemy was questionable, and after all, he would soon walk his city without his cumbersome container and more than capable, if need be, of taking care of Laxman himself. Yes, he would be happy with the character he now had strapped down – a servant of Mancirians, loyal, responsive and fully converted to the new environment that the Jaar had promised. What name fits such a splendid example of Mancirian ingenuity, Zebu asked himself?

'Dr Steel, like your new fingers, claws as hard as nails like the Master-tree's spikes and your metal hat. Here, let me uncouple the tubes from your top plate. Dr Steel, who is your master?'

'You are, Zebu Manci.'

Zebu was delighted. 'Then go and inspect my city, control my Lairs, and report back what you find. Stay clear of the Jaars till I introduce you to Laxman, their leader.'

Dr Steel's assessment thrilled Zebu. Its information detailed and efficient – the number of Lairs still functioning, the number of dead thrown to the Chutes, the number of Jaars, the state of the city's buildings and Rim rails, the burnt-out Library and its destroyed lab, the Master-tree and its spreading saplings shooting up around the city, perfectly emulating the tree, and how the Jaars were converting Lairs inside the Mancirian ship so they could function in the new atmosphere – all information that Zebu already had. Yet he was well pleased with Dr Steel's report and his no fuss-manner.

Even Dr Steel's introduction to Laxman had gone without a hitch. Laxman just said, 'I understand that you need a head Lair. But we Jaars find them obnoxious to work around. Their cold body fluids, flicking screens and reptilian fingers repulse us.' He was about to say *as do you Mancirians*, but clenched his jaw.

Zebu could not have cared less. The freedom he'd found in escaping the dome over-rode everything. He would tolerate Laxman for the present. The Master-tree was indeed a marvel that he himself could understand. After all, they had something in common. They both derived their nourishment from the same source, even though Mancirians preferred theirs decaying and liquefied.

Then Dr Steel told him of a tree out in the far reaches beyond the snail cages, which were abandoned and destroyed. There were no stocks remaining of Callic Dimension 5, the Lair continued, no datura plants existed and what snails he'd seen were crushed. Their shells littered the grounds. It found only one Halflight – rotting flesh, a tongueless foul-smelling ancient – that it put to compost.

'Your Lairs have repaired the Rim rails and cleared the streets of damage. The Jaars are fitting conductors to the overhead chutes into the Undercity, remarkable machines that process the carbon dioxide back to oxygen, a perfect system, impressive. The city has been stabilised. Laxman has been most meticulous; supervising the installations himself. His tree needs fresh meat to survive and the only source he has lives in the Undercity.'

Zebu impatiently cut in. 'What about this tree you have found. Is it one of the Master-tree's offspring?'

'No, nothing like it. It's quite different in colour and shape, covered in leaves and much larger than the Master-tree, and it's pumping out oxygen, not carbon dioxide.'

Zebu tilted his head back to peer past the high-rises. A brooding cloud blanketed the city, fingering the turrets, already collecting black streaks of crystallising tar. The sticky yellow haze that clung to the pavements and the swirling mist as it vaporised was drawn skywards and consumed inside the bleak slate canopy.

Zebu's head felt giddy. He squared it to his shoulders and the mechanisms of his brain danced in their cradles, sending electric currents down through globules, percolating the fat that wobbled in chain-reaction down the length of his body. He flexed his talons, opened his mouth, and flicked out his tongue.

'Keep your screen on Laxman. The Jaar wants to rule our planet and he will plot ways to nullify the Mancirian governor-ship. Dr Steel, they intend to make all Lairs redundant, surplus to requirements.'

The Doctor's screen rolled and its metal fingers expanded. Their tips – sharp, pointed daggers – glinted under the dull lights of the Metropolis. Zebu lent down and tapped its hat. 'You will always be needed in the Mancirian Empire, my pet. Now, go bring me the tree you have told me of. I have a place for it in my empire.'

Zebu could see Laxman approaching. His movements were sleek and full of economy, light-footed, the opposite of Zebu's own bulky awkwardness. His sooty-yellow eyes scrolled rapidly, as his thin arms led him forward. He raised his bony fingers to brush back fine strands of hair behind his tiny ears, covering a flap of skin which protected the gills that generated his own biosphere – an aura of carbon dioxide encased his body.

'I see you are enjoying the carbon dioxide, free of your tubes and container. Let's find a place to talk,' Laxman said, leading Zebu toward the control room, Dr Steel a few paces behind.

'No, alone Zebu, without the Lair.' Zebu dismissed the Doctor with a wave of his talons. 'You have work to do. Go do it, my pet.'

'Does it know its life is terminal, that the carbon dioxide wreaks havoc with their plastic and tin, their converters only a stop-gap to get a few more rotations out of them? They are an unwanted breed, low-caste, brainless machines destined for oblivion, soon to be farmed in their human form, a larder for the Jaar Empire.'

'This is a Mancirian planet,' Zebu screamed. 'Your place in it is fragile. The alliance has yet to be fully ratified.'

Laxman's eyes narrowed and he took a step backwards as Zebu exposed his sharks' teeth. Tea-coloured gunk dripped on to his tongue, which he swirled around his ballooning cheeks. A reminder to the Jaar of the Mancirian volatility.

'What is it you need to talk about? I have little joy in your company and I have an important mission to finalise before the ship's launch for Manci.'

'Your anger is uncalled for. My interest was in your well-being. We have installed a vat inside this wall,' Laxman said. 'Look behind you. See? Your hosing and tubes lying in their cradles. You no longer need to pump your food from the bowels of the Undercity. It's on tap right here and we will keep it well stocked with the most decayed bodies we can find. It was agreed that we would work co-operatively. We have fulfilled our side of the bargain. The Lairs will be phased out. Besides, it will be a natural process. They can't survive the elements of carbon dioxide. As I say, it is a perfect solution. We won't need them. They're unstable. That was your downfall in the first place. That's why we are here. To revolutionise your tired old systems. Will I send back a dispatch to my commander saying that the Mancirian plans to revolt?'

Zebu let out a long, frustrated 'Nooo. Laxman, Mancirians are true to their agreement. But just one thing, I want Dr Steel kept alive. As a pet, you understand.'

'You can have your pet. The rest will be phased out. No more Lair conversions. Acheron Afrit does not live on plastic and tin. The All-knowing-One desires true flesh. Your craft is about to depart. Are you ready to give it clearance? We can watch it depart on the monitors.'

The roar of the engines igniting filled the city. Flames leaped, blistering the pavement. Buildings rocked, twisting on their foundations. Lairs cringed from under whatever cover they could find, as the packed control room of fifty-odd Jaars and one Mancirian looked on in silence.

* * * * * * *

Dr Steel and its small army of Lairs ceased their chopping. They felt the earth beneath them tremble as the Mancirian ship shot overhead, trailing a stream of fire in its wake. The screens of Oak's tormentors craned skyward, their tools limp in their menacing fingers before recommencing their deadly attack. Gross sounds, grunts and laughter seeped from their voice boxes as each bough crashed to earth with a dull thud.

Oak was drained of fight. Her flaying limbs, severed, bleeding, fell in ever-increasing numbers at her feet. The Lairs scrambled, climbing inside her canopy into places she could no longer protect, places her branches could not fold back on. It was a massacre. Each wretched swing of the axe rang out across the compound that once held memories of light, love and hope for the Lairlights, the Kuaha and all humanity. Her leaves were shed like tears, carpeting the graves of Ubu and the Kuaha warriors.

She stood brutally amputated, stripped bare, staunching her own bleeding. Residues of resin quickly formed across each cut. Like a colony of termites parting her trunk from her roots, the Lairs feverishly hacked away. She braced her heartwood as Dr Steel pulled the wand from his jackboot, buzzing, glowing in his rapier claws. Her stump was mercifully cauterised by the searing wand.

* * * * * * *

Silk grabbed at her chest, her heart pierced by the thunderous noise of the Mancirian craft departing and the chaos of people crying, screaming as the Undercity walls swung, threatening to topple. Objects bounced from shelves, tables skidded and crashed together. A wave of revulsion spread through her body. Beads of sweat broke out on her forehead. Then a vision descended on her, stamping itself inside her head, of a great wounded tree being dragged through the streets of Lair City and dumped unceremoniously at the foot of the Library steps. And around the tree stood Lairs, their screens rolling, looping, illuminating the tortured bark.

* * * * * * *

Zebu strutted towards Oak with a swagger in his pumped, quivering body, his clawed feet clicking at the pavement.

'You have done well, my pet. I want it placed at the top of the steps upright and made in the image of me! So all who pass by will know Mancirians rule this planet. That even the trees bend and shape themselves in our name. The Jaars will learn Mancirians too, have a tree. They will press their heads against its feet with offerings from

Acheron Afrit, switches from its saplings.

'My tree is hungry too, hungry for the respect and devotion that I demand. It is Zebu Manci that gives them shelter, a place to dwell. Make sure, Doctor, I am not disappointed with the likeness of me.'

When Laxman heard of Manci's machinations he thought Zebu had lost his mind. He found Zebu standing ramrod-straight in the portico next to one of the massive columns that supported the Library roof, posing with his right claw pushed forward, his head swollen with pride. He wore a long-sleeved jacket that looped over his head. It fell, cascading down his chest in scalloped folds, echoing the fat globules that ringed his waist; a skirt of jelly protected his legs, from which his ostrich-like feet clung to the slab floor. Many small tubes weaved to various parts of his body, looping over his broad shoulders and connecting to a reservoir – a casket of fermenting human body parts that bulged on his back.

Dr Steel continued carving, his rapier fingers slicing away chunks of Oak's wood. The twenty-foot replica, twice Zebu's size already coming to life, dominated the portico.

'Are you mad, Zebu?' Laxman enquired, his voice barely holding back his rage. 'Have you lost control of yourself? Jaars will never prostrate themselves before your image. Acheron Afrit's limbs are sacred. We worship only the Master-tree. The all-knowing one.'

Zebu dropped his claw and shuffled forward to meet Laxman's words. Dr Steel ceased its work, turning its screen to glare at the Jaar, brushing wood chips and shavings from its full-length leather coat. Its bladed fingers clicked together like shears.

'Lost control? How can I lose control of something I already control? You are here to co-operate, not dissent. Jaars will also worship Cirian, the Mancirian tree. You will be first to place a twig of Afrit and bow your head at its feet. See? Already Afrit has given up a part of itself to Cirian.' Zebu's voice boomed, waving an arc with his talons towards the first step.

Laxman's head almost exploded. 'How did this come about? No Jaar would perform such a sacrilegious act.'

'Dr Steel has many fine qualities. His fingers stretched and he clipped a branch. Your tree did not object. Would you like him to cut a piece for you?'

Laxman's face turned red, his eyes scrolled as his bony fingers scratched at his forehead. He was simply dumbfounded, astonished that a piece of Acheron Afrit lay at the feet of the half-finished idol.

'The problem with you Jaars is you think yourselves indispensable. You think Mancirians are reliant on your Master-tree, captives of your technology, and so must follow your superstitious religion. Only one tree? Hah! Take a closer look at what I now wear – a Mancirian design, not Jaar. With this pack, I can generate my own carbon dioxide while I derive nourishment. You see, your tree is not needed. Mancirian minds are elevated, capable of the most advanced science. I do not have to fear oxygen. I can travel, walk through the Outer-world, go places your tree could never reach. Dr Steel was most helpful in its construction. He has such a sharp mind.

'Dr Steel, what do you think? Tongue in or out?' Zebu flicked his foot-long tongue out. It scrolled past the Jaar's eyes, over his head.

The Lair, skipping on the scaffolding, yelled back, 'Tongue out, Master.'

'This is outrageous,' Laxman managed to blurt out.

'Not at all,' Zebu retorted. 'Your tree multiplies. It can afford to applaud Cirian's existence, give a part of itself and I decree that all Jaars will acknowledge our tree or you will feel my wrath. I expect to see your Jaars coming to pay homage as soon as Dr Steel has completed my likeness.'

Laxman was defeated. The Mancirian's power was waxing as he spoke. 'Jaars will not rape Acheron Afrit. Your Lair will have to do the trimming and even if they are forced to touch the feet of your ugly piece of dead wood, their actions will hold no reverence. It will be false praise. There is only one Master-tree.'

'Now there are two. Cirian is hungry for the Jaars' respect. Be sure you are the first to show it, Laxman.'

Acheron Afrit

Chapter Two

We strike out for the Kuaha village. It must be a struggle for the Lairlights, their cumbersome, awkward bodies a hindrance.

Chief Otahi, frustrated by the slow progress, drops back to talk. 'Solo, it's clear the Lairlights will find the journey difficult. My warriors are eager to see their village and there is the painful task of telling families they have lost their loved ones in battle. There will be great sadness. Weeping will flood our houses. I will leave Nua with you to make your way. I will take Jall. I think it best to separate the two of them for the time being. Nua can be so unreasonable. Pig-headed. He spits out Jall's name like poison. My brother has a bee in his feathers, a buzzing that seems to have confused his heart. I was hoping you might try and chase that bee away.'

'I understand. Nua is my dearest friend and I believe you are right to keep them apart for now. The Lairlights are weak from lack of nourishment. I will have to find a way to feed them. I've been thinking about this problem.'

'Solo, the Kuaha village will be a place of mourning. Bitter and dark. Some may not take to the Lairlights. It's a heavy price we have paid for their rescue and that of the Undercity folk. Some will want retribution. It will take all my power to convince them I have made the right decision in bringing the Lairlights into our lands. I will have trusted men keep watch for your arrival. It could be a disturbing experience. Keep them close when you reach our fields. I have promised them safety and a place to dwell. I will need the Ahorangi's blessing.

'I should have sought this first before making such a promise. I worry I could have overstepped my mana. Although I am Paramount Chief, the leader of my people, that does not give me the automatic right to bring aliens onto our lands. You, of course have Neke as your companion and as such you are valued. Your prestige is without question. My people think of you as Kuaha, as I do. But be prepared for insults and protests, even direct challenges. There will be those who will only be appeased by reprisal.'

Otahi grabs me firmly by both arms and presses his nose to mine. In his tattooed face, I see the seriousness of his words. His eyes say *believe me, this is no idle banter. Pay heed.*

He turns to trot back up the trail, then stops abruptly and calls, 'If you find us greeting you in the company of the Ahorangi, your safety should be assured.'

It is a moment of sober reality the Lairlights and Undercity humans have yet to face. We labour all day down the ridge. I glimpse the set of boulders that Bella, Race and I recovered beside after we had crossed the Great River on our first excursion into the Kuaha lands. A crippling pain wraps my heart when I think of Ubu playing with the children and the fierce loyalty we have lost. I curse Smelt with each step.

We thread our way towards the base of the hill, the Lairlights stumbling, tripping, cursing as well, a nasty sound that reverberates in their bowler hats. Each step drains what energy they have left. The flax shoulder bag Nua made me cuts into my shoulders. The rattle of acorns taunts me with the folly of my claims of a solution to their fate.

I begin to think the Lairlights will not make it to the village anyway. Their feeble movements are now just a crawl, their screens barely emitting a glow, their fingers – bruised and battered from breaking their falls – retracting in their gloves.

The Undercity folk have fared better but they too are finding the constant uneven terrain troublesome. It is a silent march across the open grassy flats to the boulders of my past, where I said we would camp for the night, where food and water can be found. At last we make the citadel of rocks. It is torment to rest here. I concentrate on the task at hand. Nua goes off to find wood and kindling, taking Cullum with him. He is proving to be helpful, no longer the rabble-rouser Nua flattened. His freckled face is swollen and one eye blackened, his ginger hair is littered with leaves and twigs that he picks out of his unruly locks and tosses into the stack of kindling.

He has drunk water from the tarn a short distance away in the woods, and he excitedly tells his clan of its existence. They all descend, parched, greedy for its restorative gift.

The Lairlights sit propped by the rocks, wasted. Their screens drop to their chests, a panting sound escaping through their voice boxes. Nua and I lumber up the rise to the berry tree that Race and Bella so happily danced beneath, squirting juice and seeds at one another. The first smile of the day creases my lips as I remove my coat to make a bag for the fruit. Together, we bring back our pickings.

'This is the first place I ever saw the creature Smelt,' Nua says. 'It was on its hind legs, by the boulders when it caught my scent. Its rage demonic. I was with Powerflower. We had to retreat. It still sends pangs of fear into my soul just thinking of it.'

'It's dead now,' I reply.

'That hideous thing claimed many lives. Many of my own people, and the Lairlight Zappa and the miracle dog Ubu Aroha.'

'Please Nua, do not speak of it. Or else I will weep a river that will not stop.' Deflecting the conversation, I continue, 'I'm going to crush up these berries into pulp, add some water and pour it down the vents in the top plate of the Lairlights. I'm not sure if it will work. Their stomachs have been fed on a cocktail of Manci's creation. I hate to imagine what a putrid concoction it was. Will you help me?' I ask Nua as we approach the camp.

'Of course, Solo. I heard your promise.'

The Undercity folk met us, their eyes popping at our bounty. I feel mean of spirit when I say the berries are not for them, that they will have to forage their own, that these are for the Lairlights. I point to the tree on the rise. They can see the orange berries still in abundance, bunched, hanging from the boughs. They set off in a rush towards the tree. All seventeen of them babble with joy, ecstatic in the knowledge that their stomachs will be filled. Watching them climbing in the tree's branches, devouring the fruit, I have a nervous feeling that maybe they will wipe it clean of fruit, but I am pleasantly surprised. They take only what they need.

I saw the Lairs' top feeding plate when Dr Hasame made me watch the demise of Jip and Mace. But I had no idea if the solution was heated, or what it contained. I guess now it would have Callic Dimension 5 crushed up along with snail slime and datura. I could only offer watered-down, pulped berries. I wonder should I remove the skins and seeds, and which Lairlight I should use as my test case.

I eye up the forlorn group. They all look shattered and beyond help. So I move towards the nearest one. I expect to be beaten off, or some reaction at least to my hands breaking the lock that connects the hat to its screen. I ask Nua to hold down the arms as a precaution. As I remove the hat, a small puff of smoke and a mouse-like squeak drifts into our camp. The screen shuts down completely. The Lairlight looks dead. Now its top plate is exposed and I can clearly see the hole where I have to deposit the nourishment.

I set to work quickly, using the bowler hat as a pot in which to crush the fruit while Nua breaks the thread of another, using the hat to carry water from the tarn. It spills through the voice grill as he races back to me. I add the water to the pulp. It smells sweet and alive with goodness. My hands are sticky and stained. Holding the hat above the top plate, I pour in the liquid – skin, seeds and all. I'm not the least bit sure how much I should give each one, so settle for a quarter of a hat.

By now the entire group of Undercity folk are milling around, startled by the nuts and bolts of these poor creatures. Human, just like themselves, trapped by genetic engineering in which I played a shameful part. I finish the last pour just before the light fails. Cullum has set the fire. I am warming to him more as each hour goes by. Now we can only wait and see if the Lairlights will accept the offerings.

I find a place by myself among the boulders as Nua takes off into the woods. I have my head between my knees, staring vacantly at the ground between my feet, when I spot a piece of cord-like rope, then more and more of the stuff, and I realise it is part of Bella's old shoe shredded by Smelt. Just the knowledge that the beast had been here makes my insides turn. Morose thoughts, tangled emotions of regret, a savage plague of disgust overwhelms me. A reel of memories flicks through my brain as I turn the rope over in my fingers.

I feel trapped, like the Lairlights in their cages, trapped inside my promise to make them whole. Trapped inside Nua's struggle and his hatred of Jall. Trapped inside the idea of saving the Undercity beings from the Aliens. Trapped inside Epic's words, Powerflower's kindness. Trapped in the vision of Silk walking away from her possible freedom. Trapped in the horror that is war, mayhem, death. Tears run down my face, splash onto my fingers as they fiddle with the string.

And Oak, that beautiful tree. No, more than a tree; an identity, a spirit, delicate yet tough. Trapped in Jall's decree that she would be eradicated. Trapped in my union with Neke. Neke! Where is she? I haven't seen her since our arrival at the boulders. She'd wound her way down my arm and disappeared.

I want to melt into the earth, be done with this stupid quest. What is right, what is wrong, who is evil, who is good? I simply want to dissolve, become one with the air and evaporate. Locked inside my bubble of sadness, I feel I can no longer step up to my responsibilities. Why me? Why do I have to carry such a weight? My shoulders burn from the bag of acorns, my heart still aches for the loss of Ubu.

'I'm tired,' I mumble to myself through my dribbling nose, which I wipe across the back of my sleeve. 'Tired of the frightful endings. Where is the joy I felt when I first managed to talk to Bella and Race, the elevation I knew when Epic revealed himself, or when Keywee pranced, and Powerflower flew into my life? Why so much destruction and loss of proud warriors? I am no more than those that now sit around the fire, an Undercity being brought above by Manci, a drone to work for his ends, a shell of a human who has seen far too much to ever feel real again. There has to be more than this – a better state, a state of grace.'

And it is while I am thrashing around inside this abyss that Silk's face penetrates the cloud that fills my mind. She is smiling. Her calmness and her beauty are unfathomable. She holds out her hand and says 'Solo, you will discover the journey is within, not without. Do not look for it in the world, it is in your heart that it resides.'

I could swear she is whispering in my ear, that she is squatting beside me in the shadows of these rocks. She also says, 'Be gentle with yourself, Solo. Fill your heart with memories of love. Stop beating yourself with the bitter rod of what you can or cannot change.'

I stop crying, truly believing I feel her hand touch my forehead. Peace such as I have never known envelopes my being. My body feels a profound warmth, as if a skein of impenetrable silk-cloth has wrapped my skin, a protective coating that cannot be disturbed, and in that moment Neke appears between my feet and climbs up my arm, saying, 'She is quite something, that girl. Full of wisdom and knowledge.'

Then Nua appears out of the night, grinning. 'I have a treat for us,' he says, holding out five large trout that he says he tickled into his grip. His laughter is like falling stars – the kind you wish upon, a private wish. One you must keep close or it will not come true.

I fling myself to my feet and embrace the Kuaha while slapping him on his back. His smile broadens as he says, 'Come on, let's cook this manna from heaven. My mouth is impatient for its flesh.'

We sit by the fire and Nua entertains the group with his stories of calling the fish to his hands as the smell of trout blends with the smoke and wafts into our nostrils. The Lairlights however, still propped, each screen blank, only reflect the flame of the campfire back at us. We eat the fish, share in its bounty jollied by the sound of fingers being licked clean. Even Neke partakes in the feast, delicately accepting the small chunks from my greasy palm.

Suddenly, some of our group start pointing and their voices lift a notch or two. There is excitement like that of a flock of startled birds. I turn in the direction of their gestures to see two of the Lairlights' screens pinging, scrolling and looping, glowing the orange colour of the fruit I administered. From within each screen human features peer back at us, and their gloved digits are normal now in size. They are pulled to their feet by the Undercity folk and embraced, all babbling, talking at once.

Now the night holds a magical quality that sweeps all of us into euphoria. It is a miracle beyond description. We dance and holler until fatigue compels us to camp down and sleep. I pull my bag of acorns close to my body and watch as Neke curls up in it. *The Guardian*, I think, as my eyes shut and Silk's words cascade through my body – *the journey is within, Solo.*

I wake several times during the night to see the Lairlights huddled in a group, their screens dully glowing, quietly chatting to each other. I hear snippets; talk of their new-found health and recall how the berry juice soothed their linings, improved their vision. A deep feeling of satisfaction settles over me as I drop off again.

* * * * * * *

Still, our progress is slow. The hill tracks are laced with roots and stones, puddles and mud, obstacles the Lairlights find difficult to piece together, forever apologising for their inadequacies and lack of co-ordination.

Each evening, I crack the threads and remove their bowler hats to pour the juice into their thankful frames. By the fourth day, we all realise the change is permanent. We are fascinated by their evolution as parts of their boxes – their cages – start to change colour and corrode, chip and break away. Their awkward, oversized bodies start to shrink, human definition ripples under their coats. Their voices lose the brittle pitch that vibrated out of their hats.

We make our last camp high up on the plateau. Mt Cloudcatcher, dressed in snow, watches over us. Now we will easily make the Kuaha village by noon tomorrow. I am cheerfully supervising the Lairlights into mushing up their own meals when Nua comes, asking for a moment alone. He leads me down the track to the edge of the stream.

'My people know we are here. They have been tracking us. Otahi would have prepared the way. But this does not mean that these refugees will be accepted. Our system has its own codes and some of our warriors will be steaming mad. They will want trophies of heads to satisfy their pain. They will be hungry for blood, reprisal, payback for their own loss. I will be stunned if it is not so.'

I had been floating for the last few days, daydreaming of a life without complications. Nua's words smash my peace, shattering my visions of Silk. Her face sinks deep into the stream, to be swept away towards Lair City.

'Jall will be there, worming his way into my brother's heart. I have tried to trick myself into believing I am wrong about him, but nothing has changed. I do not trust that evil piece of shit. All I ask is that you keep yourself away from his counsel. It will bring about your downfall, and of any who mix with him. We have been through many difficult battles and we have always watched each other's back. That is all I'm doing now, watching over your life.'

'Nua, your bother has asked me to talk to you. He believes you are mistaken about Jall.'

'Hah, my brother. Once, he would never have questioned my instinct. He would have followed me to the ends of the world through the fires of hell. Now he ridicules me, treats me like a common slave. Can't you see how Jall has woven his lying tongue around my brother's mind? It is not Kuaha to treat a foreigner better than your own.'

'So this is your problem?'

'Solo, don't say that. I need you to listen, not make judgements. I do not wish to become angry with you. What about Oak's acorns? Why did he have none? And truly, ask yourself, did you see Jall in Lair City actually fighting the Lairs? Did you not notice how clean his coat and boots were when everyone else's was covered in oil, blood and muck? Stop and think about this. Isn't it convenient that he is the only human not fully converted? How did he survive? Where did he get his food? How did he go undetected? Did you see him fall on the bridge?'

'Nua, Nua, this is too much for me right now. He was too far away for me to see him at all. I have listened and I will take heed. And if it makes you happy, I will keep well away, but I have a more pressing concern and that's what awaits us at your village, for Chief Otahi has told me the same. He did say however that if the Ahorangi was with him, we would be safe upon our arrival.'

'He has over-simplified this. Although none would dare cause a quarrel while the Ahorangi was in our company, it does not mean they won't when he is out of sight. All I can say to you is to be careful. I will try my best to keep my eyes open. Voices will have been raised. Some more vocal than others. Their hands will not be far from their clubs and not even you are safe if a blood debt is to be avenged.'

'Nua, you are scaring me. I wish no harm to anyone. All I wish to do is convert the Lairlights and live a life without struggle, to know peace, see Bella and Race, Count Keith and Angel Cupcake again.'

'It is not my intention to cause you grief or fear. It's a forewarning of possible events. I will always stand by you, Solo. You are Kuaha. I will keep my thoughts of Jall to myself and try my best to help you find your peace.'

* * * * * * *

The sun beats down upon our heads as we enter the Kuaha gardens. I have the Lairlights packed close together, surrounded by the Undercity folk. Nua leads us in. I walk directly behind him. The path is lined with villagers on both sides, some boo and sling abuse, others bare their buttocks directly at the Lairlights. The closer we get to the village, the more compact the crowd. Neke wakes from her slumber and wraps my arm, her head reflecting the sun off her scales. Many step back and drop their eyes to the ground as she swings out towards them. Others turn their heads away. Many young warriors poke out their tongues, hiss, and mimic the Lairlights' walk, while pounding their clubs against their thighs.

The Lairlights are spooked and jittery, turning their dilapidated screens from side to side. Their fingers retract in their gloves. I lie by saying this is a traditional welcome, but I am fooling no-one. It is outright hostile.

We see Chief Otahi, the Ahorangi and their guard moving towards us with Jall tucked in behind, dressed in Kuaha fashion with top knot and head feather. It looks out of place on his white face, his white legs rattling his flax skirt, his hand clasping a wooden club and for the first time a shudder slips up my neck and I think perhaps Nua is right. Jall is not to be trusted. He is the only person smiling. His face holds a smirk. One I'd seen before. The one Nua had desired to wipe from his lips. The lines of Kuaha press forward. The Undercity folk are being pushed and spat on. I urge them to stay calm.

We are greeted by Chief Otahi in his finest feathered cloak, his face set firm. The Ahorangi looks frail and walks with the help of a staff. His dignified head held high, his white hair, falling over his shoulders, devoid of adornment.

When we connect, Neke stretches across the divide and travels with the Ahorangi. My heart takes a leap. I want to cry out to her, *please don't leave me*.

Without a word, they turn and lead us down the track to the Meeting House. The throngs follow. Now we are encased by a closing net of Kuaha.

Chief Otahi and the Ahorangi mount the steps and stand on the verandah of the Meeting House. Otahi beckons Nua to his side and they press noses and embrace. Nua bows towards the Ahorangi. I am requested, and nervously I join them. The Ahorangi holds Neke above his head so all can see her. She scans the crowd then wraps herself around his neck. Her tail falls down over his bare chest. Then he lifts up his arm and bids me to do the same. Our fingers interlock and Neke makes her way across his forearm as she had on our first encounter, intertwining both our bridged limbs. The crowd falls into a hush. The message is clear, that I am a brother to the Ahorangi, my position in the village unassailable.

'Nua has returned with Solo and Neke. They have brought with them those that need our friendship, those we have spilt our blood for. Here they are,' Otahi said, spreading his fingers in the direction of the Lairlights and the Undercity folk. 'You discredit our dead if you continue with your protest.'

A voice yells from the ranks. 'They were not worth such precious blood.' A surge of voices join in unison. 'They are not human, not of this world.'

'They are human. Look closer. You will see their true selves. They are victims of the Aliens. They are what you will become, all of us, if we do not banish these Aliens from our world. As I have told you, your hatred is misplaced. It should be directed towards the city I have described to you, across the Great River.'

'The Aliens you speak of. They have not come here. They do not trouble us.'

'How quickly you forget the demon Smelt. It crossed the Great River and soon other monstrous creatures will do the same. Then you will suffer the damning boxes these humans of the low lands are suffering.'

I lean into the Ahorangi and whisper in his ear. He holds his staff high, then lowers it. The crescendo of voices drops with its descent.

'Solo will speak to you,' he says, and he steps aside.

'These creatures are human,' I tell them, 'and I will prove it to you. If you give me the chance. Epic of the Superbird Race has charged me with this task.'

'Epic is a myth, a story. We have never seen him. The Sansvira are long gone.'

'Who claims such?' Nua screams. 'Show yourself. Your voice is like that of a rat, hidden in tall grass, knowing it has a hole to hide in.'

A stocky, broad-shouldered warrior parted the crowd, pushing his way through the Lairlights to stand at the foot of the steps. His skin is the blackest I have ever seen. His top-knot holds many feathers and his eyes flash white within the complexity of his tattooed face. He plants himself, spreads his legs and crosses his arms. One hand holds a greenstone club. 'I do,' he says in a strong voice.

Nua's body tightens. He is about to spring forward in challenge, but Chief Otahi holds him back.

'Ahh, Rangi. So you doubt the word of your Chief and his brother, of Solo and those of us that have laid eyes on the redeemer Epic.'

'Yes. They are stories to keep us in place, under your yoke. You grow fat with pride and authority, then you fill us with stories we have no way of confirming, and you want us to give up our lives for this myth. I am not alone in my stance; you will be disturbed to hear. But you can't hear, for you are deaf to your own people.'

Nua's rage is now such that his whole body shakes. Still his brother holds him back.

The Ahorangi hobbles down the steps to confront this upstart. He says nothing. Not a word. Though he is a good foot shorter, he squares himself up to Rangi and once again lifts his staff. Rangi edges away. The Lairlights scatter, screens flickering. Rangi spins around and shoves aside those that prevent his retreat.

'Run to your hole, you shitty little rat,' Nua screams. 'Who else among you questions your Paramount Chief?' he bellows. 'Now is the time. Show your miserable carcasses.'

'These creatures have my support and my promise of a safety within our lands. You will see that they are of flesh and blood, and any who see it in any other way have this moment to voice their thoughts as Rangi has,' Otahi calls.

Night will soon be upon us. The villagers stand in the shadow of the meeting house, the bickering and harassment drying in their throats, their anger subsiding. Everyone is waiting for the next person to speak. They shuffle from foot to foot, a little bored, kicking at the dust. They have heard enough. Then, from out of the doorway of the Meeting House, an electric blue pulses. Suddenly, the crowd finds its passion again. It ripples through the crowd like a wave, their voices surge together into one cry of amazement. And Epic strolls through the Meeting House doorway to stand next to Chief Otahi. Then he moves down through the throng, directly to Rangi.

'I am Epic of the Superbird Race, friend of the Kuaha. …but I forget myself. I am only a myth.'

Rangi drops to the ground, grovelling at Epic's tail feathers, tears trail in the dirt as he crawls on his hands and knees, stripped of his dignity.

Nua yells 'Run, Ratty, run.'

Epic then strolls back to the Meeting House and vanishes inside its dark doorway.

The Kuaha disperse to their dwellings, some shame-faced, others full of joy and elation. The crisis averted.

I look across to Otahi as he expels a lungful of air in relief. Jall loiters by the post that holds the roof in place. Nua glares at him. Neke leaps from my arm to follow Epic. The Ahorangi turns and also follows.

'Jall, you will take the Lairlights and the Undercity folk into the fields. Camp down by the stream for the night. Tomorrow we will sort things out, find them a spot to build their own dwellings. I will have my guard join you for safety, though I feel all will be secure,' Otahi says.

'Should Solo not also be with us tonight?'

'No, I have need of him and Nua. Do not be troubled. The sight of Epic will fill their minds and their conversations. It is a blessing he arrived when he did. Come Solo, let us discuss the future with Nua my brother.'

I remove my old boots and follow Otahi into the Meeting House. It is as I remember, the main pole carved in the images of the Sansvira. The Ahorangi, deep in conversation, is illuminated by Epic. Neke is wrapped around a nearby pole.

The huge space of the Meeting House echoes back our footsteps as we make our way forward, collecting ourselves in a circle facing Epic. His ethereal blue is the only source of light, and it bounces off our astonished faces as he tells us of the state of Lair City and its new arrivals, the Jaars; of Oak's felling and her torturous conversion into the image of a Mancirian. It is hard news.

Then he tells us how the Master-tree dines on the meat of Undercity folk; how the air is being converted to carbon dioxide and that it will soon be impossible for humans to survive inside the city; how the Master-tree's roots spread and produce perfect replicas of itself; how it will eventually creep across the Great River to lay claim to the Truthstream; and how we will then be over-run by Jaars and Mancirians.

'We'll stay vigilance over all new trees that push their way into the Kuaha sky,' Otahi said.

'It is worse than I have told you. Zebu Manci – for that is what he calls himself – has developed a jacket which manufactures carbon dioxide. This means he can move about in your land whenever he wishes. It is the same for the Jaars, who can provide for their own needs as well.'

'Then we are finished. They have won,' Nua says.

'No, not if you still have Oak's acorns in your care.'

'Yes, I have,' I blurt out. 'I still have to find the formula that you spoke of to free the Lairlights. I think it won't be needed though. The berries they devour have begun the process. Already they are more human than Lair.'

'Their use is not for the Lairlights, Solo,' Epic says, 'Oak has told me to plant them within the city, that they will grow at the same pace she can, that they will flourish, self-seed, and replicate acorns by the millions. Then the Lairs came and sliced her apart and well, now she is on the library steps. But listen, the Undercity still exists and they have oxygen. I have heard the voice of Silk. She communicates with me.'

The Ahorangi broke his silence. 'Silk is an oracle. She has contacted me as well. Her spirit has walked this house, though it could not hold her for long, I know she is trying to reach us.'

I am flabbergasted. 'That is amazing,' I chirp, 'for I have felt her too. She has spoken to me, relieved my troubled mind of the horrors we have survived.'

Without warning, Nua pounces across the room and collars Jall.

'What?' he says, 'are you a spy as well as a liar?' And he flings Jall at the feet of Otahi. 'See? Here is your friend Jall, sneaking like a fly into your larder to turn it rancid.'

'Jall, explain yourself before I end your life,' Otahi commands.

'Dear Chief, I only return to tell you that your requirements have been fulfilled, that all is well with the Lairlights. I thought you would wish for this report.'

'How long have you been in this house?'

'I only just arrived when your brutish brother attacked me.'

'Get to your feet and hear this once, and once only. Never come into this house uninvited. Do you understand? Your presence has violated the most sacred rule of our people. You are forgiven this time because you are ignorant of this. Now, leave before I lose control over my brother.'

'I will make sure he does,' Nua snorts, and man-handles Jall to the entrance then slaps him hard across the cheek. 'You have dirtied your own nest,' he laughs. 'You will be sprung in a trap of your own making and you will not escape, dog's breath. Your cunning, devious plots will be seen for what they are – self-preservation.'

Nua watches from behind a post on the porch to make sure Jall does not turn back. 'Evil worm,' he mutters to himself as he rejoins the gathering.

'Let's not quibble over Jall, brother; I'm sure he was just trying to please me.'

'That's crap, as you will see some time very soon.'

'Nua,' Otahi growls. 'Forget your personal dislike of Jall for just one day. We have more to ponder on than the life of one survivor and warrior from Lair city.'

'Otahi is right,' Epic says, flashing his brilliant eyes, a sight seldom seen.

'No matter what you believe or think, we have no choice but to go to war with the Aliens. They plan to take this earth for themselves. Do not underestimate what I am telling you. This is not about you, or you,' Epic says as he unfolds a wing in my direction. 'It is about the future of your children. Your whole realm is in a perilous situation. Humanity's future is at stake.'

'War and death,' I exclaim. 'Is that all there is to this life? I'm sick of it. My life has become meaningless. No better than it was when I worked for Doctor Hasame and Zekai Manci.'

'Solo, you forget what your life was like, drugged to the eyeballs, blindly running after Manci. You were a puppet, a slave of the Alien's world. You forget what freedom means, the cost one has to pay for such truths,' the Ahorangi says.

'But it's the same prison,' I reply. 'I'm a slave to this conflict. That I'm more aware of its workings doesn't help.'

'We will succeed, Solo. It's just a matter of commitment, of freeing ourselves from these awful fleas that suck at our bones.'

'Your part in this has been set in time,' Superbird intercedes. 'After all, it was you that brought Bella and Race to bring about my birth. Remember this. We will defeat them, Solo. Have faith. You are still needed. To what end is yet to be revealed, but believe me, you are integral to the cause, just like you were when you first escaped the clutches of Lair City.'

'Hey smarty pants, you with the blue suit,' Neke purrs. 'Go easy on my friend.'

I am shocked back into myself. These are the first words I have heard from Neke for an age. They break the impasse and somehow we all find ourselves chortling at Neke's humour.

'Then let's contemplate a strategy, a way forward,' Otahi says.

The Ahorangi speaks and his words are measured. 'It's through the Undercity that we can penetrate. I will meditate on reaching the woman Silk. She has the gift, the power of astral travel, the ability to bend matter, to infiltrate the ether. She will reveal more than we could discover by ourselves.'

'I can hibernate at will,' Neke says, 'so I can live above ground in the city for long periods until one of Oak's acorns strikes, then I will dwell in its fauna, move from sapling to sapling till I can understand their Master-tree and its weaknesses. Let's start from the snail cages, where the foliage still stands, and we can progress slowly towards their stronghold. They haven't destroyed these, have they Epic?'

'No, they're still intact though derelict. It's a good place to start. The Desert of Circles is sand and steel. No tree can live there.'

'Then it is from there we will make our stand,' Neke proclaims.

'And we all agree we will fight,' the Ahorangi says as he pulls from his pocket a light that glows violet, as if he has captured a star and hidden it away. To our profound joy, Powerflower materialises in front of our eyes. This, of course, brings immense happiness to the heart of Otahi, who almost leaves his body.

'Powerflower, oh Powerflower,' he rejoices as the flower expands to light the corner and bathe us in the pure colour of hope.

'Dear Chief, you are worthy of my presence, as each of you are. I, too, have ways of infiltrating the foe. Their evil ways must be obliterated. It is humans we seek for our world, who will care for our gifts and bounty. Keywee sends this message to all things that care. These evil times have brought her forth. She too, hears the earth pleading for the very life of all that is good. Your fight is not alone. And I have the fauna and flora on my side. The earth has shaken itself awake.'

* * * * * * *

Rangi wallows in his own misery beside some reeds by a stagnant pond of water that infects his lonely bed. Mosquitoes swarm, revelling in the offerings of his tormented disgrace. Fixated on the recurring thought of revenge, he slaps and swears at an infestation of itchy sores, scratching and tearing his skin till he is covered with his own blood. The continuous, droning, high-frequency buzzing of the mosquitoes echoes the frenzy of his mind and his loss of mana. How can he walk his village again without people tagging him with Nua's words? They will taunt him and they will say *there goes shitty little rat*. Now he welcomes the bites. 'Here, feast on my body,' he moans into the night, 'come, dine on my rat's blood,' he whimpers. His self-loathing is complete as blood poisoning spreads throughout his swollen body.

He grabs at an idea that no sane being could have conceived of: Otahi has set him up. Epic is no more than a costume, sewn from the feathers of a kokako and worn by a human. The illusion fooled the village. It spoke in a voice he now recognised. It was the voice of one of Otahi's guards! Why didn't he challenge the bird?

He will make Otahi confess, and the village will declare Rangi the Paramount Chief. The people will welcome his wisdom and leadership; his status as their most fearsome warrior. Otahi, not Rangi, will be here along with Nua in this swamp. He will bind them together, drag them here and stake them to this spot to be eaten alive.

* * * * * * *

The village wakes slowly in the perfect dawn. The call of the tui rings out across the fields. There is a nip in the air. Otahi is determined to settle the refugees into their own allotments, to move them out of the village. He knows not to flaunt them in the faces of his people. He is heading for the Meeting House to ask the Ahorangi his thoughts on the best location for the Lairlights. He is greeted by women making their way towards the gardens; others squat at their cooking pots preparing the morning meal. A dog is scratching and chewing at its fur, chasing fleas, its teeth make a sound like pebbles being rolled together. He passes warriors stretching, yawning in the first rays, his purposeful stride leaving their greetings in his wake. I race to catch up, buttoning my shirt on the move.

'Good morning Chief,' I call through a dry mouth, a pace or two behind. Otahi looks around but he keeps walking.

'Ahh Solo, go fetch Jall. Bring him to the Meeting House. I have work for him. Now, Solo, don't loiter.'

Veering away, my arms open wide, like a wood-pigeon, I cheekily reply, 'At your command, Chief Otahi.'

It doesn't amuse him. He keeps his pace as I peel off, soon returning with Jall, who is eager to cajole me. He talks of his blunder of the night before and complains yet again of Nua's antagonism. Brushing away a pesky fly that has followed us across the fields, I tell him to forget it.

Otahi is alone, waiting outside the Meeting House, impatient to get started. 'Jall,' he calls, before we even arrive, 'I have made my decision where to place the refugees.'

He is down on his haunches, drawing a map in the dust, when out of the corner of my eye I see Rangi moving around the side of the Meeting House. His hair is matted and covered in mud, one hand feverishly scratching at his blood-stained arm. He looks demented; a crazed glaze fills his bloodshot eyes.

'Here comes Rangi. He doesn't look too good,' I say.

'He's coming to apologise,' Otahi replies without looking up from his diagram, which Jall is busy studying, bent at the waist, leaning over Otahi's shoulder.

Rangi doesn't look to me as if he wants to make amends. I am mesmerised by his deplorable state. Then I watch him pull his greenstone club from under his cape and raise it above his head. I can't quite trust my vision, and then he breaks into a lurching run.

I scream out, 'Otahi!'

The chief lifts his chin as the club is about to split his skull like a melon. I stand a pace away, frozen to the spot. Jall flings his body over Otahi just as Rangi's club is about to punish him. It skids off Jall's scalp and smashes into his hand. I hear the sound of bones breaking and the unholy howl of Rangi cursing Otahi.

Otahi rolls away onto his feet, bringing his own club in an upward arc to crash under Rangi's jaw. I hear it shatter. His teeth explode from his mouth and his brain rattles in his skull. Blood pours from his ears and a puzzled expression flicks across his eyes. His hands jerk at his side, his club dances, held by a string around his wrist, then his whole body convulses and half his tongue falls inside the torrent of black ooze around his feet. He collapses into a heap, wriggling in the dust, wiping out Otahi's drawing.

Jall, who had been knocked unconscious, starts to come around. He feels for the lump, then realises his fingers are useless, crushed, mangled. His good hand grabs at the twitching digits, then he lets out a loud cry of pain. Otahi, on his knees, helps Jall to the Meeting House steps. Nua and Otahi's guards arrive.

'Jall just saved Chief Otahi's life,' I stammer to Nua as the raucous sounds of concern and inquiry fill the air. 'Rangi tried to kill him,' I blubber.

Otahi's guards circle Rangi's body, kicking it till it is unrecognisable, looking more animal than human.

Jall's hand is shaking like a leaf, his face creased with agony.

Nearby villagers also come running to see what has happened, and with them comes a woman of healing who sets about caring for Jall's injuries. She lays him out on the verandah of the Meeting House while Otahi hovers nearby.

'Be off with you. Give me space,' she says. 'He will survive. Leave me to my work.'

'Be sure it is your best,' Otahi demands, as he shuffles away. He finds his brother and says, 'You had better review your feelings about Jall, my brother. He has shown us the measure of his courage. Now I'm indebted to him for the rest of my days.'

He turns to me and says, 'You will have to help the refugees this day. Nua can help you after he has disposed of this dog.' He kicks at Rangi's body as he departs down the track, his guard, somewhat ashamed, following closely.

* * * * * * *

Several weeks into their relocation at a plot on the other side of the stream, about a mile from the village, it becomes apparent the Lairlights will indeed reclaim their human selves. They pick away their screens like sunburned skin. Three of them are females, the other five male, all at different stages of their lives. The juices of the berries miraculously reverse their fortunes. They are a timid lot who keep to themselves although the Undercity folk include them in their society, but they never regain their human dexterity and their movements are still awkward, a little spastic. Their hands stabilise, yet they are still abnormal. They never complain, and learn how to grow crops and forage for berries, a diet that almost entirely sustains them. The settlement consists of half a dozen dwellings clustered closely together.

The Undercity folk take to the land, building in Kuaha style, helped by Otahi's craftsmen and gardeners.

I envy their peaceful existence. They are always pleased to have my company, but my visits become more and more irregular. 'Solo, friend,' they say, 'why has it been so long?'

Jall's hand recovers. The fingers on his left hand are bent, incapable of fully stretching back. He is given his own dwelling in the village and never crosses the stream to visit those we once considered his own ilk. He is the one hundred percent white warrior of the Kuaha, always greeted with respect and reverence, with the beginnings of a facial tattoo. He is now inside our plans of war against Lair City, privy to the most intimate details of our hopes for victory. Nua holds his tongue, but withdraws more and more from our dialogue, spending more time away from the village than in it. I am sad about the distance he keeps, and I find myself pining for his company.

Then the day comes when he announces, 'Solo, I'm leaving the village for good.'

'What? What do you mean? This is your home. All you hold dear is here. Your chief, your people.'

'I need to commune with myself and with nature. I have thought about it for some time.'

'Where will you go? Can I come and visit?'

'No, not…well, not just yet. Give me space. I have much to contemplate.'

'What is the problem? No, sorry, not problem. Why, and what do you need to contemplate?'

'You know the answer to that question already, Solo.'

'It's still Jall, isn't it?'

'Yes, it is. He still troubles my heart. And I have no solid reason to feel this way. Still, he is a thorn to my nerves that pricks away each second I see him strutting through our village, sitting in council, hearing our plans. If I stay I will cause no end of trouble. I will disgrace myself.'

'Nua, we need you to help carry out our plans. They are nearly complete and action is called for.'

'I will help when and where I can. You will hear of my exploits, see my work. Our paths will cross. Solo, I will return when my heart has been corrected.'

'Well, tell me where you are going.'

'No, Solo. Just let my brother know what I have told you. He will understand. It is what he would do if he felt as I do.'

I walk with him to the edge of the gardens; I watch him disappear down the track. It is like losing a limb. An emptiness sinks through me as I drag myself back to the village. I wait until the next day to relay Nua's thoughts to Otahi, out of earshot of Jall. At first he is angry, but he soon calms down.

Most think nothing of Nua's absence as he has been coming and going so much of late, but a few close friends, warriors who survived the battle of Lair City, ply me for information. I make sure to omit his struggle with Jall, but I sense that a few of them already know of his objection to Jall's meteoric rise within the Kuaha ranks. And, in fact, I notice how they keep their eyes fastened on Jall as if waiting for him to slip up, to show his true colours.

* * * * * * *

I spend days isolated, overwhelmed by the idea that humans are essentially alone, victims of their own fantasies. Struggling hour after hour, freezing cold, beside the tarn on the plateau in the ranges behind which the sun sets, throwing its long-fingered shadows across the Kuaha village thousands of feet below. My teeth click against each other, tapping out a secret language known only to themselves. I pull my coat closer. My head complains of the cold, a jig dancing out the emotions that dissect the shivering landscape of my heart.

I have come to the tarn to see the cairn of rocks that Bella and Race excavated, rolled away, to expose the egg of Epic of the Superbird, to talk to the wondrous brave tree whose tentacle roots had harboured Epic, to smell the perfume of its exquisite flower, to gain courage for yet another assault on Lair City.

To my disbelief, all that has survived in that gale-swept frozen eerie is a pool of ice and the burial mounds of the fallen Kuaha, which at least affirmed *Solo, you're not going mad, yes, this is the place, yes, we fought here for humanity's welfare and future.*

The nights are long and the star-filled heavens light the door to my tiny bivouac, a crude collection of leatherwood branches and tussock that moans a forlorn tune as the wind strums its structure.

The departure of Nua has thrown me into a morbid state, and each time my eyes fall on Jall my brain hurts more and the desire to find Nua increases. I search in places I think he might have removed himself to – deep dells, bends in the river, places of koura, trout and eel, his favourite foods. All to no avail, until I find myself here in need of confirmation of my past, only to crash in its desolate greyness and bitter chill, stuck with my rattling teeth and flapping arms that work feverishly to circulate my congealing blood.

Promising myself I will leave at first light, I find myself still circling the tarn to watch it crack, fracture, melt in the midday sun, free to ripple and reflect Mt Cloudcatcher across its surface. Then it is chained again by mind-numbing cold and frost, sheeting it over as soon as the sun has departed. I see it as a metaphor of my own life, my present situation, trapped by the coldness of death and war. The moments of victory shallow and fleeting, as I question my teeth for answers they had locked away in my clenched jaw. The taste of the smoked eel, dry in my mouth, once a great pleasure now seems a duty of survival. Food eaten alone is an awful business. I try to evoke images of Silk, to lure her to my campsite, pleading with the mountain air to bring her my way, to bring down on my poor spirit her wisdom and warmth, her stillness, her love.

I screech at the moon, scream for comfort, understanding, insight. I throw rocks at the sheet of ice that rings my feet hoping it will crack, relieve me of my prison, unlock the words that wrap me in this limbo of nothingness. The rocks only skip across the frozen surface to disappear. How evil the world has come to be. An ungiving, desperate hell that is going to smother us all, drag us down and beat the truth into us.

Even Neke has abandoned me for the rafters of the Meeting House and the company of the Ahorangi. Count Keith and Angel Cupcake are out on the coast with Bella and Race. 'Yes,' Otahi has said 'yes, we will take you there just as soon as the world has been returned to the Kuaha.'

Jall sniggers when I tell of my quest to find Nua, calling him self-indulgent, a slacker who distances himself from his responsibilities to the people. I could strangle him in that moment, though what do I do? I sulk off across the stream to spend time with the Lairlights and Undercity folk in the hope they will understand my plight, the ache in my chest. But they are too busy giving their own lives meaning. They are happy at their rebirth, elated, dwelling in the little things that bring them untold joy. Why can I not connect, share in their bountiful delight in simply being. They want me to join in, to till the soil, forget the past, find a mate, settle down.

'But it's the future that haunts me,' I reply, 'its uncertainty, its violence.'

They just shake their heads. 'We are simple folk, Solo,' they say. I want to shake them out of their complacency and scream *You don't understand, you fools. The Aliens are coming to take your simple lives away, to feed you to their tree, devour you whole.* But I bite my lip and race away to sit alone as far as I can from the acorns I have been entrusted with, as far away from the future that has been laid out for me by Epic, Powerflower, Otahi, the Ahorangi, and their plans to which I am central.

Now my provisions are running short and still I have no idea who I am or what I want anymore. My loneliness complete. Tomorrow, I will tramp back down the ranges to the village and ready myself for a future of spilled blood, a future that enters your skin and turns it to leather so the clubs of war can be deflected. A necessary chore, impossible to escape. It makes no sense to me. I was a chemist, not a warrior. I was interested in discovery, not destruction.

Nothing seems real. I question if Epic even exists. Is Powerflower a creature I've invented because Bella said it was there? Is Keywee an imagined ghost the supernatural world has fabricated? Are the Sansvira a mirage we've conjured up together, projected onto the cliff in that forgotten part of the Truth Stream? I flog myself raw over these questions; I see Rangi, his teeth flying out of his mouth, denouncing it all as myths in front of the gathered crowds only to be silenced by Epic's arrival.

How my teeth clatter, bouncing off each other. How my eyes sting. Now it is impossible to trust my own thoughts. I have achieved nothing in this isolation. It has only hardened me to the inevitable world of scheming and conquest, to the human ambition for power, and to those that would change the comfort and beliefs passed down from generation to generation. I want to surrender myself to Manci, give myself to their tree, to finish this nightmare, this illusion of life, this torment.

Now my shaking has become uncontrollable and my tears solidify on my eyelids, to crack as I blink in my torment. The hut fills with the white steam my clanging teeth allow to escape from my mouth.

I curl into a ball, clutching at my knees. The tangled limbs of the leatherwood press in. The tussock swings, throwing dark horny devils above my head that reach for my soul. I bleat like a lost lamb in a cell of my own making, unhinged, wallowing in my loneliness, wretched, preparing for my own end, stiff, unable to thaw, brittle, ready to snap in two. If I could just unfold, sink back into the miserable life that should not have progressed past the Library of Lair City.

My mind ceases to work, as if a rod has been cast amongst its cogs, bringing its unfathomable ticking to an end and I fall into a blackness I fear, yet embrace.

Then the most wonderful peace settles over me. I dream of a raging fire that warms my world of friends I hold dear – Nua, his even teeth pushing forward a smile so broad I think I am in heaven; Bella dancing with the Count; Race with Cupcake.

But then my consciousness struggles with a weight that suddenly presses down on me, uncalled for, uncomfortably suffocating. I am worried I'll be compressed into the very earth that separates Nua and me, and I find myself trying to fling my legs into the air. My complaints ring out like a bell banging against my ears, or so I think.

I wake with a strangled scream and my mouth is filled with feather-down and a thumping heart beating against my side. Scared witless, I force my head from under its weight to see the trumpeted face of Keywee staring at me with a cross expression of a kind I've seen before. She pushes my head back as if she were tucking an errant chick under her protective wing, then settles her body over mine as I stretch my legs and find a place to poke my nose into the frigid air. The temperature rises in my veins even as I accept the fabled bird's existence and mutter her name.

She rises with the sun and finds her way out of my hide, turning to stick her trumpeted head back inside to blow a reveille that shakes the tussock coverings and forked branches, not to mention my grateful ears. I crawl through the opening a changed man, ready to lay laurels at her feet, only to find her gone, as if I have dreamt her alive, as if I have fashioned her beak myself to call me from the dead.

Chapter Three

Silk, in self-exile, meditated. The futility of man's desire to rule other men, their lust for control, she understood to be born out of fear. She had witnessed their greed, watched it cripple their spirits. They neglected their inner selves. Cruel, savage and ignorant, transparent in their lies and deceit, floundering in a festering filth of their own making. It hurt and saddened her. If only they could touch their higher selves, use their minds, expand their hearts, fortify their souls, see beyond their mortal coils, past the hell of the Undercity and their daily needs. Then they would realise that there was more, that their destinies were interlocked. That they should nurture and protect each other, see the light in love.

Silk denied all requests from the Elders to see her. She was polite to them, but her words were sparse, economical, to the point. She wanted to be left to her own devices, to stay removed from the ways of the Undercity, cloistered in a private peace she had built for herself that she treasured, found inspiring, ideal, devoid of distractions. She did not want to enter the world of men – harbingers of doom – and refused to meet Campbell, whom the elders had said protected the people and shared all he had.

She said she'd found it inconceivable that the people called for her, believed her to be their Oracle – a direct line to Neke and Epic of the Superbird, in whom they saw their redeemer, their champion, their path to a better life, to freedom. A spirit outside themselves, a spirit that was not human but knew their true souls. And more than capable of rescuing them from the Undercity.

The people sent the Elders to plead with her to save them. It was a mantle she did not want. It troubled her. It seemed like a curse that would unravel her serenity. Until now she had managed to send the

Elders away each time they had arrived asking for her wisdom.

But at last they found a way to delaminate the layers she had so painfully welded together. She had been at full sail in the ocean of nothingness, transcending the walls that surrounded her, detached from the worldly ways of the Undercity. But when Elder Ottis, in his frustration, accused her of being selfish, it rocked her. And she dropped her sails to find herself circling a vortex that pulled at her safe passage, sucking her into the needs of Mt Paris and its people.

And she replied calmly to Ottis, 'I will come and investigate your claims for Campbell and the evolution you speak of.'

Outside her dwelling, she was mobbed. Campbell was called upon to clear the way. His men spread their arms to form a protective barrier keeping the delirious crowd from their Oracle. They chanted her name. Like a bushfire, word spread throughout the levels.

The stairwell soon jammed with devoted followers who relayed the scene to one another as best they could. The flow of human traffic one way filled the great meeting hall to capacity. She ascended the steps of the circular platform from which Marvin Shanks had once delivered his proclamations and handed down his perverse punishments in the course of his despotic rule.

The air electric with excited chatter, the crowd in awe of what they believed to be a Divine Presence. The Elders followed Silk and stationed themselves in an arc of reverence; heads bowed, hands clasped together. Ottis stepped forward to quell the masses and like a wave retreating back off the sand, their voices abated till silence filled the hall.

Silk lifted her face to look out across the field of heads that stretched beyond her vision, waiting to hear her words. Into the vault she softly spoke only three words. 'Love one another.'

A ripple effect boomed out within the city, as each head turned to spread her simple advice, repeated down the alleys, dancing down the stairwells onto each level.

'Love one another,' the crowds called.

Then Silk asked to be escorted back to her dwelling, accepting help from Campbell who offered his hand as she descended the platform's last step. Their eyes locked and in his she saw kindness and clarity. Qualities which she had thought she would not find in such a man – a warrior, a warlord of the people.

His hair was spiky, cropped close to his scalp. She could see a healing scar still raw from battle near his temple. She found herself smiling into his large and rather doleful brown eyes. She was impressed by his clean-shaven face and muscular frame. She thanked him. Campbell and his men formed a chain around her, deflecting the hands outstretched to touch her.

Ottis followed. 'Silk,' he said, 'will you receive Campbell and some of the Elders for counsel? There is much for you to hear and there is much we wish to know.'

'Yes, Ottis, I will. But give me a few moments to collect myself.'

'Of course Silk, call us when you are ready.'

Campbell was shocked at the sparseness of her abode. The absence of objects that littered other homes of the Undercity. *How lonely a room*, he thought as he gazed at the small cot hugging one corner, just inches from the floor, and a single chair from which hung a towel, a table that held a washbasin, comb and nothing more, and a shelf crafted into the legs of the table that held a cup, a bowl and wooden spoon. The room echoed with each rustle of her garment. Her sandals she had left at the door. He noticed her tiny bare feet padding the concrete and felt embarrassed plodding in wearing his heavy frogskin boots. Her waist-length auburn hair, now released, fell straight, cupping her round young face. Pencil-line half-moon eyebrows of the same colour as her hair accentuated her tranquil eyes, a shade of green he had never seen before. Her beauty mystifying, captivating. He stared openly, waiting for her lips to part. He thought of descriptions he had heard, of poems dedicated to birds in flight.

'I can offer you water, it is left for me each day, but there is nowhere to sit but the floor, as you can see. Perhaps Ottis can have chairs brought for our comfort,' she said, removing her towel from her own chair to the bed.

Ottis turned to Elder Watts. He nodded and left, to return with five chairs that he arranged in the centre of her room so they could get down to what Ottis had so impatiently wanted – the chance to tell Silk of the city's evolution into something of which he was sure she would approve.

And so the short history of rebirth, of the marking of time, spilled forth from Ottis in a rush like water cascading down a fall, finding a myriad of troughs and courses around boulders, flashing and splashing its way to rejoin its path towards journey's end.

'Today is the two hundred and twelfth day in the Undercity's history of rebirth. The two hundred and twelfth dayday since Campbell convinced the good people of Mt Paris and the Undercity to stop killing each other and work together for the same goal. To share our wealth and protect each other from those who wish us evil, those that come to snatch us while we sleep – the Aliens from above.

'You have been here inside your shrine, fiercely protected, guarded by the people. They believe you are our salvation, the direct line to the outer world. Neke and Superbird paid homage by revealing themselves first to you alone and it was you who stayed behind with us Elders, knowing escape was futile at that time.

'Campbell and his men fight bravely but are outmatched. The Aliens are clever. We have never captured a single one. There is no pattern to their arrival, the door slides open and they obliterate any barricade or obstacle we place in their way. Then they send in Lairs to cut us down and abduct many of us in one swoop. Modified creatures, Lairs like we have never seen before, strange apparatus screwed to their bowler hats. It's all over in a matter of minutes. It's impossible to avoid the stairwells, our only way to move produce, materials that we share, to visit families on other levels. There is always a flow of humans close to the door. We try to keep the children as far from it as possible. People take their chances, knowing the door could open at any time. Still, they chase us through the city if they have to, confident in their superior arms and strength. Now that we know we do not transcend to a better life, we fight and defend ourselves. They have even secured one poor Elder on his way to deliver a sick mother her last rites. Many of Campbell's men have been taken, dragged kicking and screaming, through the door.'

Campbell watched Silk's eyes for a reaction. She did not blink. She sat perfectly still, hands in her lap making no response even at hearing the most gruesome details. Finally, Ottis finished. They waited for her reply.

'It pleases my heart to know you have found a way to live together and share the bounty of this world, and I can only instruct you in the ways that hold truth for me. The Aliens will keep coming. They have developed a new world above. A world no human can survive in. A world of carbon dioxide. An air so vile and toxic that one breath alone will collapse our lungs, burn our eyes, choke our throats. They come for us to feed a tree. A tree I have seen in visions. A tree that they worship, and call Acheron Afrit. It eats us whole, alive or dead, it does not matter. It is this tree that converts the air into carbon dioxide.

They are farming us to feed this tree.'

Campbell grabbed at his mouth. Shock dug into his spine. The Elders all turned to look at each other, stunned by Silk's words.

'So we are doomed, like frogs in a tank, waiting to be plucked for the plate. But in our case, fodder for a tree,' Ottis said, under his breath. 'And even to escape would mean certain death above in a world we no longer know, or can survive.'

'No, Ottis. The Truth Stream still exists and the Kuaha rally, as we speak. I have heard them in my dreams. I have seen Epic and Neke in the Kuaha Meeting House discussing their plans. There is with them a noble man of spirit, ancient and wise. He has come to me and whispered *have courage, have faith*. And also the one named Solo whom I know to be a key figure in their success. I have met him in the flesh, by the feared door to our underworld. And he too reaches out to me in search of peace.'

Campbell coughed. A fever raced through his head. A tinge of jealousy to which he had no right. *Solo*, a name he had heard before, bit at his skin. He moved in his seat, crossed his legs and looked at his boots, ashamed of his unruly heart, which he knew he had already lost to Silk, the angel of his dreams. A woman he would willingly die for.

Silk looked across to him, caught his eye as he lifted his head. He felt pinned like a moth to a wall. He felt her reading his heart and shyly coughed once more, hoping to distract her from her digging.

'There is one more thing I should tell you,' she said as Campbell regained his concentration. 'It is the story of Oak, another tree that has been at the forefront of my mind. A spirit I can touch, which abhors the Aliens. A tree from the Truth Stream that dwells in Lair City and wills its collapse. A local tree, a representative of all the species of trees and flowers and grass. The exalted example of the gift they have given humans from the time of creation – oxygen. A tree that eats carbon dioxide, and celebrates its victory with fruits and leaves, and multiplies itself for its love of balance. A tree so feared by the Aliens that they had her axed and ridiculed and shaped into the form of the Mancirian Zebu. A tree he believes he has tamed, condemned to the glory of his own ego on the steps of the Library in their realm. A tree with memories and the ability to commune.'

Silk rose and shifted her bed, pulling it from the corner to expose one lone root that had cracked the wall of her dwelling resting in a small bowl of water.

'See?' she said. 'Come, touch its glorious limb. It lives, projecting all its energy into the Undercity, relaying the sorry state of our planet above. A conduit of information, a stream of knowledge. It was through Oak that I found the courage to join you all again. It is because of her I can tell you there are two races of Aliens above, in conflict with each other. Of the antagonism that sizzles between them; Oak plans to be of use in this quarrel. She plans to survive. And so should we.'

The room filled with the sound of chairs scraping the chilly floor. The Elders moved towards Oak, each respectfully waiting for his turn to touch the singular root. Their faces lit in ecstasy as if they had been blessed. They moved around the apartment, embracing each other, babbling, cheered, ecstatic, suddenly unencumbered by thoughts of Aliens creeping into the world, and unaware of Silk and Campbell.

'Won't you touch Oak?' she asked him.

'If I could touch your limbs, it would do even more for me,' he replied, 'for my faith is permanent. I have seen the light that floods my heart already, and you are it. At last my life has meaning beyond myself. Still, I will touch Oak as you have asked of me,' and he walked across to the root, bent and placed his hand over its splendid finger while staring directly into Silk's eyes.

'Will you water my love for you as you water Oak's needs?' he asked openly.

'It is already being done, Campbell, though you might not recognise it, for I believe you want more than I can give. I have places to go that you cannot come and you will resent that, as you have already done this day.'

'Is it Solo who holds your heart? I sense your fondness for him.'

'Solo is my brother. A fellow traveller who questions what is right, how life spins us inside out, then outside in. He is a special human that has risked all to start this quest for liberty, freedom for our race. He is a human I'm most fond of, radical like you, honourable like you, but destined for a different future, – not with me, yet a friend for all time.

'No, Campbell, my heart is not ready for this world you propose. I have duties beyond coupling. Don't be disturbed, please do not feel rejected. I love you now as we share this space or any space the universe allows us to occupy. Attractions fade. You will find this to be so. You are a man of substance. I do not ridicule your advancements, but I must set them aside for my world is full at present of unexplained currents, contacts that need to be upheld, interpreted, unravelled. I have no time for romance that could waylay, or interrupt, this necessary flow.'

'Thank you Silk, I understand. Will you tolerate my proximity? I will guard you for all time.'

'Campbell, I do not need a guard. I am looked after by Oak. You must continue as you have. Guard the people from those above who would have us tamed and ready for slaughter, a gift for their abominable tree.'

Campbell straightened, ran his hand across his head; disappointment tugged at his lips. Lips that were about to protest, suggest she was wrong, that she did need a personal guard, but then realised it was a selfish need of his own, that its purpose was to be close to her, drink in her beauty, smell her hair, fathom her grace, bask in her tranquil, moon-shaped face, drown in the depths of her eyes.

He watched Silk now gently bringing the Elders to order, rounding them up, gesturing to them to be seated, smiling at their bewilderment, as they returned to the bodies they had left while in their euphoria.

'I left the Undercity to walk in the Truth Stream,' Ottis's voice said in a wondrous tone. 'I saw mountains, rivers, the sea and trees filled with birds, all singing praises to the sun, people tending flocks and gardens. They recognised me, bid me a pleasant day.'

Elder Watts bounced in his chair as an excited child might do, impatient to add to Ottis's tale. 'Me too,' he said, 'me too.' The others nodded. 'Yes, it was the same for us. How can this be?'

'The power of Oak is beyond explanation, though we must try to tell the people of its existence.'

'No,' Silk demanded. 'Oak's root must not be mauled or discussed. I bind you to your solemn word on this matter. You have been privileged to commune with her, to be enlightened by her nature. You may speak of her as a spirit, a vision, but her whereabouts must be reported as ephemeral. This room is a sanctuary for her growth.'

'They will want to know the outcome of this council. What shall we say?' Ottis pleaded.

'You may say to them I am a conduit, their connection to the outside world. That, yes, indeed I am touched by Epic, Neke and Oak, and that they deliver their blessings to the people. They work for our release and promise us a future in the sun. They are exalted by the harmony and kindness the people show each other. Humanity will be rewarded, their faith sung inside the Truth Stream, their belief a lantern that will light their way. Their future shall be built on a foundation of love.

'You must not jeopardise or compromise the safety of Oak's tendrils. The throngs that would descend on this room will destroy the silence which allows communication.'

As always, Ottis stroked his white beard as he spoke. 'Your words are diamonds; they reflect the mystical, complex truths of life. We will do as you ask. It will be enough for them to know Epic acknowledges our prayers.' Together, the Elders stood and bowed their heads.

'Campbell, please stay a moment longer,' Silk asked as the Elders gathered the chairs to depart. 'I have changed my mind. Your guard will be welcome. If you would station it by my door it would be a wise precaution, so I am not disturbed and that Oak's life force is not discovered by the curious, or an innocent victim of passion moved beyond their own control. Campbell, you too I will hold to your word. Oak's secret must stay a secret.'

'A guard will be at your door at all times. No-one will ever enter on any pretext. Your sanctuary is safe, as long as I breathe, and my word is my bond.'

Silk lifted her hand and stroked Campbell's cheek. A rush of warmth flooded his body. 'Thank you, dear man, your words flatter and bolster my spirit. I'm not totally lost to this world. One day, if the universe permits, we may stroll the Truth Stream together but for now it is impossible. I am contained, happy with my lot. My need to serve consumes my life, awake or asleep. There is no other cause.'

Campbell left, backing out of her apartment. He felt he was walking on air, born anew. It was, however, a spell broken immediately outside Silk's door as a melee of Undercity folk crowded in on him. They had surrounded the Elders, who were still pressed for news of their council. Quickly, he organised the watch, his orders precise and drummed into the men who soon cleared Silk's doorway.

Drawing a line in an arc on the floor and pointing to it, he said, 'No closer than this shall any being come. Do your duty with diligence. You must remain here at all times. You will be relieved in rotation. Keep your wits about you. Be forceful but fair, kind yet firm. Silk wishes for no gifts. She has all she needs.'

'What of those who are pilgrims, those that have travelled from the Levels bearing offerings for which they have sacrificed, gone without? Their hearts will be crushed.'

'There will be no exceptions. The Elders will spread the word. I'll see to it. Have them give their gifts to the needy. It is what Silk has asked.'

Each day, a new tendril broke into Silk's room, forcing her to move her bed to another corner, rearrange her meagre possessions. Each root fattened, twisted, grew till it filled the corner, then almost half her room, creating a lattice of soft wood she could slip within, caress, even sit upon or climb to the ceiling if she desired. Soon it weaved a pattern into itself, creating a hammock of woven strands she could sleep within and her cot became surplus to her needs, so she pushed it through her doorway. The Elders had it removed. Now she dwelt in Oak's domain, half way up the wall, cradled in its company, the room more a cave of nooks and crannies shaped by Oak's fantastic roots and the sweet aroma of its juices that kept her space warm and dry.

The Elders slipped requests under her door for counsel. They asked for instruction.

She was waiting for Oak to stabilise, to cease its push into her apartment, and at last Oak told her in a vivid dream that its feet were well pleased, secure at last.

Silk readied herself in anticipation of what would certainly be the Elders' dramatic reaction to Oak's growth, her massive presence. She knew they would want to be transported by the tree's roots once more. Oak advised against it, saying that her power had increased a thousand-fold, that the visions they would see would not all be pleasant, as Silk was well aware, and could not be sure she could shelter them from Lair City's atrocious ritual feeding of Acheron Afrit with living humans they no doubt had known and loved.

Oak wanted to spare them the hideous sight of screaming children thrown to the hated tree by the rampant Lairs, that found it so amusing to watch, and the devotions of the Jaars as they pressed their foreheads to its scarlet trunk and praised its sated limbs. It would be enough for them to sight Oak alone, to know Oak's life force had grown and that the Truth Stream was now readying itself to cross the Great River, to infiltrate by means she'd best not disclose.

Dressed in her hooded gown, standing outside her entrance, Silk greeted the Elders one by one, and had them slip through her barely opened door. Campbell kept guard, scattering the devoted who had been sitting for days hoping just to glimpse her once.

She expected cries of disbelief, delight and amazement, but she found them huddled close together, raising their hands to shield their sight from Oak's dominance, a labyrinth of interlocking roots. A thick mist clung to the ceiling, her apartment had a chill she had never known before, and what words were said fell flat, condensed, to the floor. The voices of the Elders trembled as they asked her for insight. No demands were made, no desire to touch Oak was expressed. They just inquired into her health, and of any news she had that they could take back to the people, and of any contact made with Epic or Neke.

Bemused by their timid approach, Silk watched as they shivered in their capes, their hands inside their sleeves, frightened to touch the tree. In fact, wanting to flee back to the world they could understand, as quickly as they might.

'Yes, yes and no,' she said to each enquiry they made.

'Then best we return to deliver the good tidings to the people who wait outside,' Ottis stammered.

'Yes,' she said, perhaps a little too chirpy, just managing to hide her giggle. She knew it was Oak's doing that the Elders cringed, their legs wobbled in fear.

'Then we'll go,' Ottis said, the words edged with relief. They backed away on urgent feet past Campbell into the Undercity to deliver their findings, assuring the crowds that Silk was safe.

No sooner had they gone than the mist and chill subsided and Silk laughed and chastised the tree, placing her hand on its thickest root saying, 'That was naughty of you. You scared them. That was not right'

'Oh, yes it was.' Oak delivered. 'It was the best I could do. I saved them the horror of Lair City and a long interview for you. Be pleased. We have important contacts to be made. I have seen Neke inside the City, curled around a sapling borne from a seed of mine. She hibernates, as still as a branch that for now resembles one of Afrit's young and will go unnoticed for a time. This means the Kuaha, Solo, Epic and others steady themselves for the fight. I have seen Superbird flying high above the towers, above the carbon dioxide. He is planting the acorns by dropping them from the sky. Clever bird. A remarkable strategy that I'm sure he will repeat. My children will have their roots dug deep, searching out Acheron's daughters' shallow ties to the earth. They will cut off their expansion, choke their path. The Master-tree will fight back. It will be a battle of wills beneath the ground, so should go undetected by the Aliens until Laxman, the head Jaar, begins to accuse Zebu the Mancirian of creating an unstable City. Then cracks can be exposed in their fallible systems. They will squabble; neglect the necessary running arrangements of Lair City and its expanding fortress. They will bash egos against each other, and a civil dispute could give us the advantage we need.'

Chapter Four

The Orabanche slid through the spikes and thorny leaves that sparsely covered Acheron Afrit's scarlet bark. It looked a different creature. It had survived Neke's crushing coils and escaped the Undercity.

Its deformed eyes burned with malice, a red-hot memory stalked its damaged head. Its lizard-like tale flicked in agitation, raving away to itself – demented mumblings it shared with Acheron Afrit, which leaned forward digesting another corpse.

A branch whipped though the thick carbon-dioxide air, hooking the dribbling creature by the underbelly, lifting it higher to where small splayed leaves crawled with parasites – tiny blood-sucking ticks. The Orabanche's tongue slapped at the leaves, its sinister teeth stained crimson. It gobbled away at Afrit's bounty, all the time belching out obscenities, its putrid breath mingling with Acheron's foul gases.

'What a thing it is that I've found you. We were made for each other. Perfect in balance. Yes, yes, yes! You don't have to go on about it. Yes, yes, I've cleaned all your daughters, now I'm cleaning you. Yes. I've licked your bark to a buff. What's that you say? That I'm the best? Of course I am. Don't you forget that, nor your promise. That bastard snake is mine. You can have all the Undercity vermin you can devour, but that abomination is for me.'

Red slime oozed from the Orabanche's twisted mouth. It constantly scratched at itself with one hind leg, nervously poking its head from side to side.

'Here comes Laxman to suck more advice, to pray at your trunk, with some gripe about Zebu for sure. There is nothing wrong with the Mancirians. My Master is one. When I drag the body of the bastard snake to his dome I know he will welcome me. Better hide.'

Laxman bowed deeply to the tree. 'All knowing Master-tree, the

Mancirians blaspheme and clip your daughters' twigs to place at the foot of a dead grey trunk. The idiot Zebu has had it fashioned in his likeness, with his sinful tongue poking rigidly into your carbon-dioxide. He demands Jaars lay offerings of your sacred limbs at its feet and is adamant that it be done. All-knowing one, it is an empty gesture, a meaningless devotion, that you witness. No Jaar has any reverence for the Mancirian tree. We entertain the fool for the sake of the colonising of the planet. A world more Jaar than Mancirian,' Laxman begged, tapping his bony head against Afrit.

Acheron Afrit's boughs wriggled, lurched forward, above Laxman's head. The Jaar's glazed eyes, startled by a phlegmy cough, wheeled around inside their sockets. His spindly legs clicked as he jumped back a pace, his head rotating, desperate to source this intrusive sound. He walked around the tree, searching up into its limbs as the Orabanche crept around the opposite side undetected.

The Jaar picked at his tiny ears, troubled and confused by the proximity of the sound. He tilted his head to sniff, hoping to separate the deplorable gases from the odd odour that clung close around Afrit. He would like to have climbed up into the blessed tree, but no Jaar had ever considered such an irreverent act.

The Jaar was depressed, sullen. Zebu's egomania corroded his confidence. He was exhausted. He decided he must have imagined the noise. He tapped his forehead against the tree once more as a giddy rage swamped his heart. He trudged off towards the library steps.

Dr Steel's scissor-fingers pushed forward a twig from one of Acheron Afrit's daughters; his screen, popping, pinging, turned towards Zebu as Laxman snatched it from his rapier hands. Zebu strutted, flinging out his tongue to mimic Dr Steel's marvellous creation. Dwarfed by the perfect, detailed effigy, the Mancirian's body rocked, wobbled in delight to see Laxman place the twig at the feet of Cirian. The Jaar's cat-slit eyes smouldered with hate, as a bewildered collection of Jaars looked on in disbelief, huddled under the impenetrable ball-bearing coloured sky canned inside the city's monoliths.

A crystallised ooze the colour of coal seeped down the high-rise walls, staining the windows, caking the ledges in ever-increasing piles. Laxman descended the steps to join his Jaars, promising he would destroy Zebu and his stinking pet Dr Steel, who laughed as the Jaar passed.

The Jaars, moaning, in a frenzy, gesticulated towards Zebu's idol. Tears dropped from the eyes of some, a green transparent fluid.

Laxman's open mouth clamped down on his sparse square teeth. His greenish gums spasmed as foam bubbled inside each gap. 'It's a dead piece of wood that holds no life force,' he told them. 'Afrit will move to pull it apart. For now, let's amuse the Mancirian. It will drown in its own fat before too long. Gather the Lairs. We need fresh meat for the All-knowing One. Let's feed it well and pray for this planet to be made the realm of Jaars. The Mancirian has lost its mind and its diabolical behaviour will be judged by the Alliance.'

'That was a delicious moment, Dr Steel,' said Zebu. 'Did you see the misery in Laxman's eyes? The weasel wants power, wants our planet for himself. Hah! What a thrill it is to manipulate his kind. They are inferior parasites, incapable of running the worlds we conquer. Ahhh, my pet, you enjoyed it, I can tell. You are a splendid creature. I have work for you. A little foray across the Great River. Let's see how well the jackets perform. Bring my Rim. We can trolley out to the crossing. My Lairs have repaired the bridge, I take it? I need a new challenge. Let's show them who rules. Let them go off and feed their tree while we, Dr Steel, expand the Mancirian globe.'

* * * * * * *

The door into the Undercity slid up into the ceiling with a shuddering screech. The Lairs rushed forward en-masse, throttling and hacking their way across the floor of Level One, with Laxman and several other Jaars, trailing safely behind, engrossed, fascinated by the living conditions of the human sacrifices. It was the Jaar's first descent into the underworld. His gills expanded and contracted in the oxygen-rich air, pumping out carbon dioxide. An aura of gas circled his body.

The fleeing inhabitants scattered in all directions, enticing the Lairs forward, deeper into the Level, completely buoyed by the chaos they had brought. Laxman revelled in the fierce brutality of the Lairs as they relayed their victims, six barely breathing humans, back into the vault.

Laxman's confidence grew with each gangly, mincing stride the Lairs made. How impossibly easy it seemed, to capture such well-fed flesh in prime condition for his tree.

'We have enough,' a gruff voice ventured.

'No, I want more. More!' Laxman screamed as he pushed a spindly finger into the back of the Lair. 'Get moving. There is no fight in them.'

The Lair stumbled forward to join the chaos, flummoxed by the need to go deeper into the Undercity.

Laxman was smiling as he made small talk with his fellow Jaars when, to his utter surprise, the Lairs were suddenly attacked front-on by a wave of Undercity warriors. Campbell shouting orders above the clash. The Lairs, confused, drastically outnumbered and desperate to survive, began to retreat.

Rattled by the will of the attack, Laxman's ambivalence cracked, shifted into a new dimension. One of inexplicable fear, as more and more of the Lairs were forced back towards him. He could see the strained faces of the humans, flashing long spears and wielding their weapons at the legs and fingers of the Lairs, and one in particular charging without a care for his own welfare, working wildly, sweat and oil soaking his vest.

Their eyes met for a paralysing second. Laxman knew this animal was after him, trying maniacally to manipulate a gap through the Lairs' ranks to do him harm. What had been a contained situation only minutes ago now turned into a struggle for the safety of the vault and its steel door.

Abruptly, the humans ceased their pursuit. Their long spears held at full length, they were prepared to allow the Lairs to escape. Campbell at their front line was bruised and sneering. In one voice, his men yelled a victorious cry. Though they had lost some of their own, they had never had such success. To force the Lairs from their city was a triumph. Their jubilation rang throughout the Undercity as the Vault door clanged shut.

Laxman fled in a panic with his Jaars, shaken by the organised power of Mt Paris, smarting as Campbell's face burrowed into his mind. It was a haunting vision he could not erase, of a wild creature gnawing gleefully at his bones, a banshee howling for revenge.

Laxman would take solace in watching the Master-tree bloat itself on the few they had captured, imagining each sacrifice to be that of Campbell, and revising his intention to oversee the demise of the Lairs who were, after all, the ones that had to fight to procure the Master-tree's fare. This had rapidly come to seem an ordeal he was now only too willing to leave to the Lairs.

****

Zebu Manci and Dr Steel staggered across the bridge into the Truth Stream. How alien a world it was for both of them. Queer in its silence, its open sky and sunlight filling them with foreboding. Impenetrable, dense, with piercing colours of fauna and flora. It was not what Zebu had expected, and the difficulty of weaving through trees forced the Mancirian to stay close to the Great River, where the going was somewhat easier, though not without its obstacles – fallen trunks, boulders and muddy holes. They had not ventured far, perhaps a chain or two upriver. Zebu was fretful, disturbed by the trees, bewildered by their immense size and by the lack of objects, of buildings. Threatening in ways he could not decode. He sucked hard on his tubes and started questioning the functioning of his jacket, its durability in producing the carbon dioxide that would keep him safe.

Dr Steel, its iron fingers clicking, its screen looping on its constantly turning neck, was also out of its depth in such an unknown world. Still, they were here and as yet untouched and unchallenged. Just as Zebu was growing in confidence, becoming more daring and moving inland cautiously, a flock of wax-eyes swarmed inches above his head to forage in a nearby tree.

That was enough for the Mancirian, who ducked, reeling out his claws to protect his bulbous head, sending his body into a cartwheel. He groped for a nearby tree to steady his fall, only to yelp and wring his talon claw, shocked by the current that poured up his jelly-sagging arm, the pain excruciating.

Dr Steel's fingers ripped into the tree, slicing chunks out of its trunk. Zebu's legs began to itch and he stomped on the grass with his ostrich-like feet, irritated by its touch. He was bouncing on the spot, freaked by the sight of ants that streamed up his legs, screaming to Dr Steel to get rid of them.

'Let's get out of here,' Zebu bellowed. 'I've seen enough.'

And they hurriedly crossed the bridge back to his Rim. 'I want all those pitiful trees felled and this crap burnt,' he said, flicking a blade of grass from his claws. 'Dr Steel, make me a highway into this ugly land. Have my Lairs attend to this immediately.'

Zebu Manci's arm throbbed as he accelerated through the ghastly streets back into the inner city, passing Acheron Afrit's daughters. Several had Jaars loitering, tapping their heads against the bark while others directed Lairs in the destruction of buildings to make more room for the expanding trees. Their spiky boughs now littered the precinct, growing at a fabulous pace. Avenues of ghostly trunks lined Zebu's progress, all fed from one source – the Master-tree, pumping carbon dioxide into Lair City.

Zebu wondered if he touched the Master-tree, would it also cause him pain? He zipped past Laxman. The Jaar tried to wave Zebu down, but Zebu paid no attention. His thoughts were squarely focused on making the Library. His residence. A place he felt spoke of Mancirian superiority where his magnificent carved likeness stood. Would the same happen if he touched its sculpted form? Surely not. Yet it troubled him to think it might. Should he destroy all trees? They were the enemy.

He lumbered up, towards his sculpted likeness, with Dr Steel in his claw-steps. Feeling apprehensive, he gingerly placed a talon against one of the carved globules. What a relief. He then bent and grabbed at a twig of Afrit at its base. The pleasure of not being harmed bolstered his fragile state, transforming the horror trip into the Truth Stream into a victory. A heroic deed. His belligerent confidence soared as his contempt for the Truth Stream trees increased.

'I want all those trees outside Lair City incinerated, obliterated. Dr Steel, hack them apart.'

Steel chuckled. Its fingers expanded, slicing together. It was lost in revelry aroused by Zebu's words.

'I despise their leaves, their silent lives. I will have the world cleared of them and the vermin that live in and around them. Then Mancirians will have a place in which they will prosper and evolve.

'What about Jaars?' Laxman's voice called as he made his way towards Zebu, who stood under the portico ranting to Dr Steel. 'You do not mention Jaars. Do you imagine the Master-tree will stay in a world without Jaars? And then what? It's back to your stupid, primitive technologies.'

Dr Steel spun, clicking its fingers, pushing its screen close to Laxman's face. Zebu spoke: 'It's alright, my pet, go now and carry out my instructions.' The Lair's screen crackled as it descended the steps.

'What are you up to Zebu? Where have you been? I've important and dangerous news from the Undercity and you trolley around neglecting Lair City.'

Zebu sniggered. 'Important? Hah! I've been expanding the Empire. What could be more important?'

'Acheron Afrit, that's what. I too, have been increasing my power. In the Undercity. I've been down there. Have you? We were met with such force we had to retreat with only six offerings; barely enough to keep the Master-tree and its offspring happily fed. They killed three

Lairs! We were fortunate to have escaped.'

'Jaars are weak, spineless. Why we have aligned is beyond me.'

'Yes, that's right, it's entirely beyond you. We need more Lairs to round up meat for Afrit's table. Already there are reports of saplings wilting in the outskirts, deprived of the nourishment required to develop. This is urgent!'

'My Lairs are busy. We will capture a new source of meat from the Truth Stream. I have been there amongst its awful lands. Lands full of humans for its plate. No more Lairs! Send some of your Jaars down. Let them risk their puny bodies as my Lairs do.'

'That is not our strength. We are better suited to caring for carbon dioxide, tending to the Master-tree's needs.'

'Well, it's time you changed. You'll get no extra Lairs. They have more challenging work to do.'

'Then I'll send for others, Jaars who are skilled in combat, report to my command on your obnoxious, farcical approach. Recommend our departure. A full withdrawal from our alliance. Or perhaps take the city for Jaars alone. Mancirians are tyrants, uncultured in their violence, foul in their habits. Your brief rule is about to be terminated. You leave me no choice. It was always doomed to failure.'

Zebu's body shook with laughter. 'You know, I've always thought of Jaars as insects, prey for other races, easily trodden on, easy to fool. What makes you believe you will ever get off this planet or contact anyone outside of it when I control its future. Shall I show you how easily you bleed?' Zebu calmly said, ripping a line in the carbon dioxide the length of Laxman's body. 'Even on our journey here within our ship, I understood you would be a menace, a sulky bureaucrat of the alliance. I was warned by other Mancirians who had had dealings with your type to keep a close watch on you. Slippery, they said. Too tied up in their religious devotions of the Master-tree. Incapable. A folly to share power with. You'll have to harden up, if you wish to survive this Mancirian world. My patience for your interference is beginning to wilt, like your tree. You are no better than the Lairs that serve me. No, less than them, for they at least have a fighting spirit installed by our technology, not yours. So, off you go, try and reach your command. You have no chance without this,' Zebu chortled, holding a square-shaped transmitter that literally rocked Laxman.

Laxman steadied himself. 'That belongs in the control room,' he squealed. 'Without it we are locked into a void. Have you completely lost control of your position? Give that to me,' he said, snatching at it.

'See? Mancirians are not as stupid as you believed,' Zebu bellowed, dropping his talon to his side. 'You want it? Come and get it.'

All Laxman's nightmares had come at once, defeated by the tiniest piece of technology, which Zebu was waving in his face.

'Ah! Best you learn your place in my city. Fuss over your tree, bang your head against its trunk, that will keep you entertained. I have a world to tame. Just like I have tamed you, Laxman. When is Afrit's next meal? I'll come and celebrate with you. It's such a riot. All those pleading humans, screaming, wriggling in your tree's slimy branches. A truly compelling sight. I would be interested to know, will it eat Jaars? Might come down to it if supplies run low. Do you think it would know the difference?'

Laxman's face turned ashen. He opened his mouth to speak but no words could be found. Dumbfounded, riveted to the spot, with his cat-slit eyes bouncing around in absolute horror.

'And in case you don't believe me, I will throw to the Master-tree any Jaar that does not bring Afrit's offerings for my Cirian. Accept your position. This planet is mine.'

Zebu swung around, his jelly globules pushing into each other as he wobbled away into the Library, removing his jacket on the move.

* * * * * * *

'Dr Steel my pet, you're back. You look splendid. You must be pleased with your progress in the outer realm.'

'Yes, it goes well. The trees have no protection. They fall with much complaint, crushing the undergrowth and burning in ever-increasing heaps. Your Lairs are enjoying themselves. It's better than working in the Undercity, they claim. Less precarious, though a couple have been squashed by ill-managed tree-felling.'

'Laxman has told me we have trouble in the Undercity. Perhaps you should lead the next capture. Show them how it's done. Bring out ten or so humans. I'll gift one personally to Laxman; a show of good faith. He needs brightening up. Maybe I should go as well – both of us – flatten this uprising, whip them back into shape, put the fear of Lair City into their bones. Show them the true face of Mancirian power.'

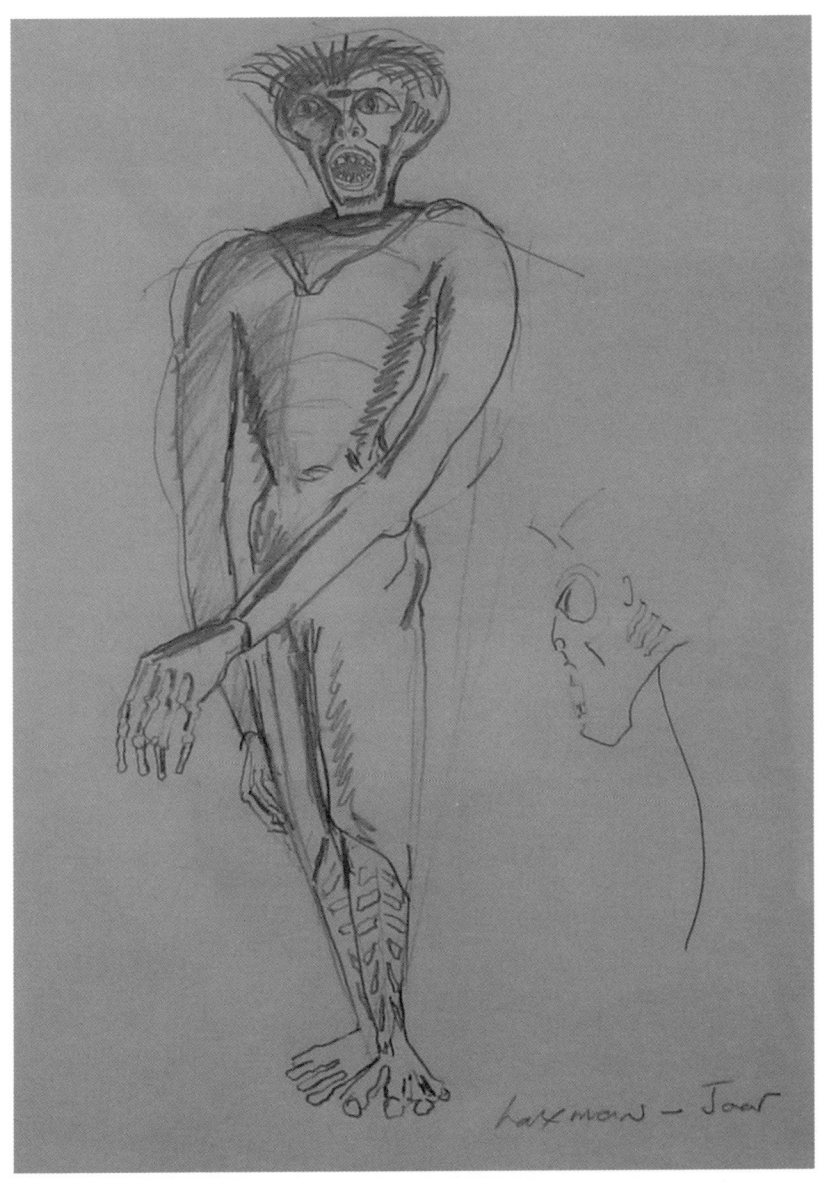

Laxman, the Jaar

Chapter Five

Zebu's Lairs mounted their perverse, destructive raids on the Truth Stream's forests, felling, burning and trampling the fauna underfoot while Oak's acorns secured their hold within Lair City. Hundreds of her saplings pushed their way into the carbon air, their roots searching out those of Afrit's daughters, strangling their growth.

It was the Orabanche who first realised the duplicity when doing its rounds, cleaning up parasites for its provider. Grumbling, bemoaning its workload, it approached Oak's offspring only to reel away spewing on the impenetrable oxygen they exhaled. Neke, tucked quietly underneath the most mature of Oak's children, was horrified to see the macabre creature sliding its way around the outskirts, licking, lunching on the nearby daughters of the Master-tree, babbling out its obscene hatreds.

A fortunate observation that gave the snake time to camouflage herself as the Orabanche coiled, writhing like a worm caught in sunlight. It flung itself away on its hind legs with a flurry of curses, back to the Master-tree to complain.

'You're neglecting your daughters, or they are rebelling in the outskirts,' it screeched. 'What's your problem? Bullshit I'm incompetent, a slacker! I slave away for you, my tongue is raw and my teeth rotten, my body aches from my tireless labour. Show some respect,' the Orabanche squealed, dribbling filthy crimson phlegm across Afrit's boughs. 'You should be fed turds. You're impossible to please. You'll never find a more devoted creature than me to groom your hide,' it ranted, twisting around the thorns. 'Your daughters are wilting and justly reject your meagre crumbs and that snake you promised still hasn't arrived. And the Jaars spend all their miserable moments bruising their heads against your over-inflated trunk.

As soon as I have that bastard snake, I'm off. Mancirians are better company.'

* * * * * * *

Neke, motionless, pondered her next move, wondering if the mad creature had found her sanctuary. The hideous, deformed lizard was a setback. She could only assume the beast would return, and surely the Jaars would soon taste the change in the atmosphere and see Oak's trees growing, strangling the daughters of Afrit.

Zebu, wrapped in his mania, either paraded by his likeness or trolleyed out to watch the hacking of the tortured forest, dragging Laxman with him to join in gloating over his dominance of all living creatures, berating the Jaar and his Master-tree's slow progress in sending its saplings to repopulate the raped landscape that now smouldered under ash.

'Zebu, the Master-tree needs more flesh to grow. Your attention should be focused on the Undercity. The expired Lairs that you throw to it are half-baked trash with insufficient meat, more tin and plastic than flesh. You have no choice but to enter the Undercity with a strong force. Put an end to their arrogance that grows each time we send down our Lairs. Pulverise the stinking humans. Stamp your authority on their entrails.'

'You!' Zebu hissed. 'Your brain has been minced by all your headbanging against Afrit's trunk. When was a human ever any match for a Lair? Your leadership is riddled with leaks. The humans are animals and, as such, smell your fear. Dr Steel will trample any resistance they offer into paste. You are intruding on my privacy with trivial problems, dispelling the joy I feel out here watching these cursed trees meet their deaths.'

Laxman's eyes were smarting in the dense smoke that swirled between them. The heat made his gills work overtime. He looked pallid, sickly in the blazing light, like a stick insect about to be gobbled up by a warty toad.

The hubbub, the raucous laughter of the Lairs, mingled with the crackling inferno. Bleeding sap bubbled at the tips of each limb, blackening the sky of the Truth Stream. Birds dropped from the sky torched by the licking flames while kiwis and other creatures fled from their burrows. They scurried past the hidden figure of Nua, crouched among the ferns, devastated and trembling with anger as the Lairs chopped a widening highway into Kuaha land.

Zebu lifted a talon and pushed at Laxman. The Jaar stumbled back a pace, gritting his teeth, then smiling as a beautiful vision filled his mind – of the Mancirian crucified, pinned by Afrit's spikes.

Dr Steel approached them, a demon rising out of the flames, blotched by cinders, its screen glowing red, its rapier fingers sizzling like hot coals as if they had just been pulled from a forger's furnace, ready to be hammered into shape one last time.

* * * * * * *

Nua, torn between maintaining his self-imposed exile or returning to his village, still hadn't quelled the pain that stabbed at his heart each time he thought of Jall. He knew his people would be aware of the fires. How could they not, with the plume of thick grey smoke suffocating the skies of the Truth Stream? His skin crawled at the idea of seeing Jall. He pulled his tattered feather cloak tight to his body, his knuckles turning white as he gripped his club. Loneliness gnawed at his bones. He longed for Solo's company, the warmth of his village. He was about to remove himself quietly from the flaming furnace and the crackling laughter of the Lairs when another mighty tree crashed, rocking the earth.

Then to Nua's utter disbelief, Jall materialised on the track just ten feet away, heading directly into the Lair's carnage. Nua rubbed at his eyes, shook his head, and questioned his sanity. Impossible. How could this be? Had his hate conjured up this vision? Was Jall really there? *I must be manufacturing this illusion. My blood is poisoned,* he thought. He shut his eyes, then opened them expecting to see only Lairs and destruction. But no, there he was, as bold as the fires, totally unconcerned for his own safety, walking into the ranks of the Lairs.

Nua pressed himself to the ground and silently crawled through the undergrowth towards a stand of tall ponga ferns. He could see Jall striding towards Zebu and Laxman, who were arguing with each other at the foot of the bridge. The Lairs ceased their chopping and closed in around Jall, who ignored them in his progress towards the demons. The Lairs followed him towards Zebu and Laxman. Now Jall was holding up a glittering metal disc.

Dr Steel was about to lop off Jall's arm to retrieve the object from his hand when Zebu moved the Lair aside. 'It's alright, my pet,' Zebu exclaimed. 'Take the Jaar back across the river. Leave me.' Laxman's protests were futile.

Zebu's massive head towered over Jall, his giant talon grabbing at the object. He scrutinised it, then leaned down and conversed with Jall, who was turning, gesticulating towards the Truth Stream, then cowering as Zebu's mighty arm lifted to swipe him across the head. But then the monster seemed to reconsider.

'Where did you get this? It belonged to Zekai Manci. I have been looking for this everywhere in his Dome.'

'I am a creation of Zekai,' Jall said, 'made to infiltrate the Truth Stream. I have Mancirian blood in my veins. Blood Zekai put there himself. He promised to take me back to Manciria and gave me this tag as testimony of his word. Zekai realised the Callic Dimension 5 was no longer foolproof, that Lairs were converting back into humans. They were known as Lairlights, and he wanted me to join their ranks, spy on them and report back to him, exposing those who rebelled against the Mancirians, those that plotted his downfall.

'So I did. I embedded myself in their trust. Now I can lead you through the Truth Stream, show you the Kuaha village, give you their Chief, if you will fulfil Zekai's promise of taking me to Manciria.'

But Zebu seemed to want more, and he kicked Jall for more information.

'There's a bird called Epic that's part of their plan,' said Jall. 'It's supernatural in some way, in touch with the land and the Kuaha, an advisor who brings back information to their Chief. I know he comes and goes from your city without your knowledge. He knows of your likeness on the Library steps. I've heard him talk of it.'

This impressed Zebu. He leaned a little closer while tucking the tag into his vest.

Nua was vindicated. His intuition had been proved correct, he had concrete evidence. Jall was a traitor, a tool of Lair City and its ruler. But sadly, he knew that he, not Jall, would be seen as the traitor if he returned to the village to give an account of Jall's deeds. No, best he kill Jall himself and live as a renegade in his own land. At least he would know the truth. Perhaps Solo would believe him.

Suddenly, without warning, Jall was trotting past his hide. Distracted by his own misery, Nua had missed the last of Jall's meeting with Zebu.

Nua watched the Mancirian cross the bridge towards Laxman and Dr Steel, who patiently waited on the other side. Then he turned to follow Jall through the forest. He knew where he would slaughter the enemy of his people, relieve him of his evil head. It would be a head-on confrontation. No ambush. He needed to catch him in a clearing so Jall could not escape. Somewhere closer to the village, on the main track where he would be found rotting in the sun.

Jall camped for the night above the waterfalls on the plateau. He seemed so sure of himself, at home in Nua's lands. It took all of Nua's strength to hold back, to restrain himself from immediately finishing Jall's life. He would wait until early morning, savouring the joy he would have, obsessively playing out the scene in his head over and over.

He must have nodded off, and he awoke to a chorus of voices, of greetings, in the earliest morning light. He scrambled over the pile of rocks behind which he had concealed himself, cursing under his breath at the sight of Jall embracing a scouting party of Kuaha. Jall's voice rose above the rest, boasting how he was on his way back from investigating the big smoke by the Great River, how the Lairs were working so devilishly hard, laying waste to the Truth Stream.

Nua was gutted. He berated himself for not doing the job when he had the chance. Now it would be impossible. His own warriors would think him not right in the head if he challenged Jall. The troop made their way noisily back towards the village, buoyed by Jall's courage in making the trip to the Great River alone; it seemed the white Kuaha's mana was breathtaking.

Nua's mind was in turmoil. What was he to do? His only hope was that Solo would listen, and for that to happen he would also have to return to the village. He would look like a dog returning with its tail between its legs. His howl of frustration echoed among the huge ancient tree trunks, as hollow and empty as he felt inside.

Chapter Six

'No, darling, Superbird is not immortal. He can die like the rest of us, and fade from the memory of men. Epic – for that is his name – is of the Superbird Race. He is the son of the Sansvira. Before the Kuaha, before our own kind, before the Undercity, they graced the skies, rivers and fields. Flew among the mountains, swam through the rivers, walked in the fields. They were the Gatekeepers, integral to the balance of all creatures. Confirmation that the world was healthy and vibrant.'

'Really, Silk? Does Superbird walk, just like us?'

'Yes, dear one, when he wants to.'

'How neat. Have you seen Superbird walk?'

'Haha. Let me finish the story. The first people to find these lands arrived in boats from across the great ocean. They were foreign to the balance of the Truthstream, and they were hungry and desperate for survival. And the Superbird Race were easy to catch. They caught them with small nooses laid out in the boughs of trees, or speared them, decimating their kind. Until the last five of the Superbird Race; these last remaining ones appeared together before the Paramount Chief of the people. He was meditating in the tribe's meeting house, alone after a disturbing conversation he had had with the tribe's holy-man, the Wise One.

'Secrets of the land had woven a delicate music in this man's ear. He had seen the future, and he appealed to the chief. He said the bones of the land were rattling, the flowers failing and the bees had deserted their hives. Eels and trout were found belly-up, cooking in the sun, and the frogs sang no more. The land had told him that his people were to blame.

'The Wise One had said, "We have crushed it with our desires and our fires, and taken what cannot be returned. We have caused great hurt and loss to our protectors, foolishly blind to their importance. We have wiped out the Superbird Race, severed the link between ourselves and Nature.

' "What are you suggesting?" the chief had asked. "Are you saying we are responsible for these things? That we have created our own doom? This is difficult to swallow, Wise One. And I need time to contemplate your knowledge. Forgive me. But I find it hard to accept. Leave me, so I can absorb this fully. My heart is breaking. Your words are heavy."

'The Wise One moved into the shadows of the meeting house, folding himself into the farthest corner as quietly as an owl landing in a tree. He bowed his head, waiting for the Chief's questions, questions he knew would come.'

'Silk, are you like the Wise One? My parents say you are our Oracle. Is that the same?'

'You are sweet to ask such a question, but no, I'm just like you. It's just that I like to keep to myself so I have more time to think. Still, the story isn't about me, it's about the Superbird Race, remember? And the poor Chief, alone, with the weight of the world on his mind.

'The Chief struggled on, late into the night, chanting sombre karakia, asking his ancestors for guidance. Then, recalling his last hunt and the state of the bush, he realised what the Wise One had said was true. Things were amiss. He squinted hard into the darkness, willing his eyes to see the truth. He held out his hands in front of his body, and like the wind blowing through the flax bushes, his fingers moved.

'Suddenly, a blue hue touched them, causing his forehead to crease. His hands now gathered in the light and cupped it. The powerful form of the last five Superbird beings standing wing to wing, upright as one, now expanded out of his palms, an extraordinary vision that pulled a frightened cry from the Chief's dry throat.

The Superbirds' eyes, full of sadness, conveyed flickering images of their destruction and the consequences to all living creatures, portents of the tribe fighting the Lairs in a hideous world of fire and mayhem. Hell itself.'

'Oh, I know how the Chief must have been feeling, Silk. When the Lairs come below, I wet my pants.'

'That's alright, sweety, so do I.'

'Hahaha, that's funny, Silk, you wouldn't do that. So what did the Chief do?'

'Well, the Chief's proud face crumbled, tears stained his cheeks. In that moment, he understood the wrong that he and his people had done, and he lifted himself up from the floor to stand face-to-face with the last five remaining Superbirds, and with a trembling voice he asked them for their forgiveness.

' "We are now the Sansvira. Five as one, one as five." They spoke together. "No longer will we dwell among you. We will withdraw into the land itself, to wait for a time when man understands that all living creatures depend on each other for balance. It is now up to you as chief of your people to lead the way. To prepare for change. Adverse times. Difficult situations are upon you."

'By now the Chief was shaking and bewildered. His eyes were wide with pain, his arms stretched towards the ribbons of delicate translucent blue that danced, fizzed, around the Sansvira, licking at the rafters high above his head, illuminating the Wise One in the corner levitating inches above his mat.

'The astonished Chief was dwarfed by the brilliant presence of the Sansvira. They'd expanded, hovering in mid-air, upright like humans, and strode around on their black tail-feathers inside the Meeting House.

'The Chief swivelled on the balls of his feet, his head moving up and down as he tried to take in the whole fantastic experience. Just when he thought they might break through the roof, they were again back by his side, joined tightly together as one, shoulder to shoulder. The Sansvira leaned into the Chief. Their eyes locked and the Sansvira smiled together as their entwined wings brought forth a large egg.

' "This is our son. Our only son. We will leave him hidden in your realm. A place that will never be found by any of your people. Yet it will be your people that will protect our egg."

'But Silk, how could the Chief protect the egg of the Superbird if he didn't know where it was?'

'Now that is a good question. Very smart. Let me continue, for that is exactly what the Chief asked, and the Sansvira said ' "We were the Gatekeepers of the Land. Now you will be. You are now the Kuaha. The Keepers of the Door. The door to Epic, our son. From this day forth you will celebrate and record this night in history on your walls and on your skin. You will redeem yourselves through this task."

'Epic's egg, in the cradled wings of the Sansvira, hummed, pulsed, drying the tears of the Chief.

' "Your Wise One will be called the Ahorangi, the Enlightened One. For it is through him we have managed to find a way to preserve Epic, the last of our race. Epic's birth will be the sign of the final upheaval and only children yet to be born, from a time and a world still to come, shall find his resting place. It is to them that the Kuaha should look towards. Human children of a different colour to yourselves."

' "You talk in riddles," the Chief stammered. "Children of a different colour, from a world yet to be born?"

' "It is only a riddle to you because you cannot see the future. It is yet to unfold."

'Then the Sansvira encircled the Chief, enveloping him in their wings, and they began to sing an intricate melody. The Chief's rigid body relaxed and he beamed in delight as each Sansvira's wing drew lines across his forehead, nose, cheeks, and chin, carving a design deep into his skin. A tattoo of history for all to see, spirals of fern and rivers, and images of Superbirds in flight. His hands reached up to trace the markings with his fingers and in the electric blue light, he said, " From this day forward, we are the Kuaha, the protectors of the Superbird Race."

'Finishing their song, the Sansvira stepped back, nodding their approval. Then, as one, they sparkled, wobbled and finally vanished with a snapping sound that trailed off to leave the Chief standing in his Meeting House, tracing the patterns on his face with his fingertips, proof that his encounter was no dream.'

'Woo, can I have a tattoo like the Chief's, Silk, can I?'

'Maybe some day, darling, but it's something you have to earn. Deserve. They're not just for decoration.'

'Silk, there you are. Hello children, is Silk telling you stories of the Truth Stream?'

'Yes, Elder Ottis. You just missed out on the most amazing story. You should ask Silk to tell it to you. Is there more, Silk? Tell us more.'

'There is a little more,' she said. 'As the night rolled over into day, the shafts of dawn's light filtered overhead, the Chief once again became aware of the holy-man in the corner.

' "You witnessed all of this?" he asked the Wise One.

' "Yes, Chief, I did."

' "So you understand you are now to be known as the Ahorangi, the Enlightened One?"

' "Yes, Chief, I do."

' "Then, Ahorangi, come to my side and enlighten me some more." The Ahorangi gathered himself, he was just about to...'

Suddenly, there was screaming in the Undercity as the steel doors slid up into the roof, people calling the alarm.

'They're here. The Lairs are coming.'

The children understood immediately. Fear spread across their little faces. Some danced on the spot, tears streaming, as Silk and Ottis gathered them together, herding them gently against the nearest wall. Armed men appeared from every nook and cranny, charging towards the barricades that momentarily held the progress of the Lairs. Campbell flashed by. He glanced towards Silk and screamed at her to move the children to the back of the hall. His face was a grimace of a twisted hardness, both hands tightly gripping his weapons. Battle-cries filled the laneways, rushing at him as he sped towards their source and his men, who stood in a packed line waiting for the inevitable clash, their spears held forward.

The barricade had been shattered into matchsticks and strewn on the floor around them. Campbell moved to the front line, calling for courage from his men, who were braced against each other waiting for the attack. Twenty or so Lairs were loitering under the doorway, their screens looping, ugly sounds escaping their voice-boxes. Campbell was confused.

'Steady, lads,' he whispered. 'Steady.'

Still, the Lairs did not attack. It was highly unusual. Normally they charged as soon as the door opened, stretching their fingers, snapping weapons, snatching at legs, throats, arms, heads – a clash that was devastating to the people of Mt Paris as they watched their own being dragged away. Heard the howling of the mangled, the pleading voices echoing throughout the Undercity. A bloody scene that no-one could ever get used to, no matter how quickly it was over.

'What's happening, Campbell? What are they doing? Why haven't they moved forward?'

'I don't know. Hold steady.'

'Let's meet them head on,' one of his men yelled, banging his shield with his club.

'No, no,' Campbell called. 'Wait. Something's not right. Steady.'

The men were becoming agitated. They didn't like having so much time to think. One threw his spear towards a Lair. It bounced off the wall, splintering as the Lairs' hideous, chilling laughter penetrated their ears. Then they parted, allowing the massive body of Dr Steel to be seen for the first time. Its fingers clicked like shears, its screen a flaming red and its booming voice rattling the door in the ceiling.

Campbell's men took a step back, stung by this fearsome creature that turned back and gestured towards something behind it. It swivelled to the side and bowed as Zebu Manci made his entrance around the corner of the door with Laxman in tow.

A moan of disbelief engulfed Mt Paris. Campbell stepped back as well, his eyes bulging in their sockets, desperately searching for the courage that was dwindling in his men and, truth be known, in himself.

'What the hell are they, Campbell?'

'It's the devil,' another cried.

Zebu's bulbous head cracked with light, his jelly frame heaved under his vest of tubes as his talon claws swept the hallway. He turned to Dr Steel and said, 'I want twelve of them. Let's show the Jaar how it's done, my pet.'

The fierceness of battle ate at Campbell's heart. Dr Steel minced its way towards them without a care for its own safety, slicing limbs, cracking bones like a cyclone, forcing the men of the Undercity to retreat as Zebu waddled along behind the monstrous carnage, giggling and extolling Dr Steel and his Lairs forward, while Laxman counted those that were being extracted in ever-increasing numbers.

'Seven so far,' he told Zebu. 'Still alive, though not whole. Try to keep them in one piece,' he demanded.

'Hold the staircase,' Zebu yelled. 'Keep them from our backs.'

Six Lairs scrambled to its entrance to block those struggling to advance from below. Campbell's men were falling around him, no match for Dr Steel's rapier-scissored fingers.

'We have the twelve,' Laxman called cheerfully. 'Acheron Afrit will be well fed.'

Campbell, with room to move now, flung himself towards Dr Steel, slapping at the Lair's boxed head, screaming with his effort, bleeding from his arm where Steel's fingers had ripped his leather. Across the hall, Campbell could see Silk and Ottis trying to calm the children who were hysterical with fear. He increased his labour. No Lair had ever been this deep into the Undercity. His men had always managed to beat them off before they advanced this far. But this was different. The Lair with the steel hat and steel fingers was unstoppable, and

Campbell's men no longer had any stomach for the fight. They were giving ground to the advancing Lairs, with only token jabs of their long spears.

Zebu Manci's head pivoted as he bellowed to his Lairs that he was happy with their catch. Then his attention focused on Silk, guarding the children. A sudden pain ripped through his body, a violent stabbing in his globules, and he clutched his claws into balls and pounded them against his chest. Dr Steel rushed to his side as Silk moved across the Vault towards the Alien.

'I've seen enough,' Zebu whimpered. 'Let's go back and feed the tree.' Abruptly, he spun around, almost knocking Laxman off his feet. The Jaar was perplexed by the sudden change of mood in the Mancirian.

Campbell and his surviving men battered, and wounded, kept their distance as they cautiously prodded the Lairs out of their city. Totally bereft of fight, believing they had seen the devil himself, they couldn't even muster a cheer as the iron door slammed into the floor with a mighty, pounding boom.

Campbell made his way back to Silk, who he found leaning her hands on her knees, assuring the children that the monster had gone. He stood a few paces away, staunching the wound to his arm. Seeing this, Silk left Ottis with the children, kissing their foreheads one by one, then glided over to help him with his dressing, pulling the bandage tight. Campbell winced.

'It will need to be stitched,' she said. Campbell nodded.

'How did you manage to do it?' he asked.

'Do what?' she replied.

'You know,' he said, 'repel that monstrous creature. It physically trembled. It was obviously in pain. It buckled when it saw you advance towards it.'

'I truly cannot tell you, Campbell. I just wanted it to know I wasn't scared. Oak has sent me visions of it from above. It is the Alien from another world I told you of. As is the skinny one. A Jaar. A different race. Come, let's clean your cut and sew it together again. It's deep and could easily get infected.'

'My men are seriously afraid of its life force. Already they talk of moving down a level. It will take them a while to recover, to believe we can continue to fight the forces from above. I've lost fourteen men.'

'I understand.'

'Silk, I need you to talk to them. Give them hope. Bless them. Instil the notion that the creature is not the devil. Tell them what it is. What they are dealing with.'

* * * * * * *

Zebu Manci stumbled up the steps towards his carved wooden likeness, disturbed, his guts churning. He felt unwell as Laxman badgered him about the girl's effect. The Jaar revelled in seeing the Mancirian challenged by a single human female.

'Go feed your tree. You have your flesh,' he snapped. Still the Jaar couldn't help needling Zebu further. 'Seems she knew you. Had no fear of you,' Laxman chortled. The Jaar, relishing the moment, smiled. Greenish gunk caked his teeth. His slit eyes rolled as he strolled away towards Acheron Afrit.

Zebu's head ached. Silk's divine features were lodged in his brain. He slumped into his chair under the Library's portico. Dr Steel helped him to remove his vest, unplugging the hosing as its Master stamped his clawed feet against the floor, working to gain control of his breathing, waiting for the stinging pain in his fatty globules to subside.

Without warning, Zebu lurched forward and grabbed Dr Steel by its coat, pulling the Lair close. He roared into Steel's screen. 'Get me one of the captives NOW! Before they are all fed to the tree.'

Steel, disoriented, tripped over its own feet as Zebu released it. It fell, landing on its knees, then scrambled away on all fours as Zebu bellowed 'I'll find out who she is!'

Eager to please its belligerent master, Steel soon returned holding a petrified human under its arm, dumping the poor soul at Zebu's clawed feet. It raked at the man's contorted body, turning him on his back. Then it took him by the neck, lifting him off the ground, his arms dangling and his legs kicking, choking in Zebu's grip. Dr Steel found this amusing. It laughed, its fingers clicked, its body shook. It was hoping its master's mood had improved.

'Filthy stinking pus. You're going to tell me all you know about the woman who looks after the children in your Undercity.'

The captive was being squeezed, his mouth was open and his face was turning black. It was then that Zebu realised it was not his throttling talons that were causing such discomfort. It was the carbon dioxide that was killing his prize. The Mancirian let out a wild, frustrated shriek, flinging the poor soul against a column, bitterly disappointed that his plan to extract information was foiled by the toxic atmosphere.

'The shitty human has already expired.'

Dr Steel's laughter was silenced as Zebu screamed, 'Get this filth out of my sight.'

Chapter Seven

A gale raged, attacking the ridgeline. Leatherwood and tussock groaned against the buffeting winds. The shifting patchwork of snow and sleet lifted in eerie swirls, tossed across the plateau, constantly rearranged into ghostly shapes, triggering a distorted, wailing shriek.

Below the summit, stunted trees bent and whipped, lashing each other, stripping leaves and twigs in the howling maelstrom. Bellowing clouds of mist cascaded, rolled within and around the peaks, fingering their way between boulders and scree, blanketing the rim high above the dell that captured the shimmering Sansvira in their towering, rock-walled exile. Patiently, they listened to Epic.

'My faith is collapsing. At first I was happy to be alive, to expel the Aliens, to enjoy my celebrity. Now it has no meaning. It is dead leaves in my mouth. I cannot live if the Superbird Race ends with me alone as I am now. Fires are consuming the Truth Stream. The trees fall and the Kuaha do nothing but protect their own needs. This is no different from what the Mancirians do. Zekai Manci's last words haunt me.'

'Son, we hear you when you say you have been contemplating the Mancirian's final words. Yes, Epic, perhaps they, too, are nature. But their nature does not suit our planet. They are better displaced, to find a home somewhere else in the universe. Not here. They are poisonous bees raiding our hive. We marvel at your ability to question, reminding us to ponder on all life forms, even the enemies of our lands.'

'Humans desire control. They too like to rule,' Epic retorted. 'There's self-importance in their greed. Humans claim a higher force than themselves, and this higher force they say has given them the right to rule. They too, lay claim to the Truth Stream, all the lands, the oceans and the sky, and they fight each other to keep ownership of its resources. A resource they abuse. This behaviour makes them no different to the Aliens.'

'Epic, we understand your position. It hurts both Keywee and I to see the Sansvira locked inside this cliff. But they placed themselves here after concealing you, for self-preservation. And yes, it was to escape the greed of humans. But it was a revelation to the Paramount Chief when he realised the forest and its creatures also needed his protection, and the Kuaha have since that day been the Gatekeepers. They have lived up to their promise. They garden our world with respect. Have faith in them,' Powerflower said.

'Faith. That's nice. Even if we banish the Aliens from our earth, I will still be alone. The last of my kind, thanks to humans. I am weary of the loss of our fabulous animals, our heavenly trees. Are their souls not just as important as that of any human? What are the humans doing? Nothing. They stand back and watch. Their time is over. The Aliens can have this world.'

Epic spun and rocketed out across the dell, circling the clearing in a flash, returning with a lotus flower he'd found in a nearby tarn. The Sansvira gazed down on their son, quietly taking in the debate.

'This lotus,' Epic said, placing it at the feet of the Sansvira, 'is a miracle that humans have not understood. They only see a flower. They haven't seen its purity, its brilliance, its evolution, how complex is its transcendence. Its life starts in the dark world of mud and ooze. It knows there's more and it struggles for the light of the sun and, on reaching its goal, bursts forth in blushing joy, in congratulatory harmony. It is a lesson in humility. The lotus is reminding us greatness can be achieved from humble beginnings; that all living things can overcome, banish the darkest moments of their lives, that we have a perfect future. We should all reach for the light. Humans are lost if they continue to see the lotus as no more than an ornament in a pond.'

'Epic, you are their redeemer. It is up to you to set them on this road. For so long now they have prayed for your return. Since the days your parents placed you in the cairn under Mt Cloudcatcher. You must not desert them in their time of need. I forbid you to do so.'

'It's fine for you, Powerflower. You're immortal. A spirit from the other side, who, I might add, held back his presence for so long from the humans. Your life is not threatened,' Superbird sulked. 'I can die! Lair city is dense with carbon dioxide, and alien creatures I find depressing. Yet I have to accept they too have a right to life.'

'I believe you are creating obstacles just for the sake of debate. I agree with that. It's healthy, but misguided. It is only you that has put a timeframe on your own life, claiming mortality. There is so much you have failed to grasp. Like your story of the lotus. Pleasant, but flawed. Not in your delivery, flawed because you haven't taken in the miracle yourself. If I've heard you correctly, you suffer from the same fears humans have. You are scared of your own life force coming to an end.'

'No, Keywee. You're wrong. I do not fear my death. I fear a life alone.'

'Where is your companion Neke? Does she waffle on about immortality, never-ending life? No. She is, right now, at the front of the struggle. Prepared. Why? Because she knows she is both the giver of life and the minister of death. She knows of the miracle you refer to. She sees more than just the flower. She also knows that there is no choice.

'Humans are capable of transcending, of elevating their spirits to a higher plane. They have been slow in their evolution. That is why they make mistakes. It is through these mistakes that they find understanding and learn that all things great and small are symbiotic to their very existence. This is why Powerflower and I have revealed ourselves and come to give aid.'

'The Truth Stream was once in perfect balance,' Epic replied. 'The Superbird Race and all creatures dwelled unharmed before the humans arrived. Humans too are aliens, and they brought with them their perverse greed. What makes you believe they are any different now, Keywee? It is said that the Kuaha arrived on our shores fleeing famine, pestilence and sickness of their own making, escaping fires of destruction and death from other lands. They had started wars against others of their own kind. Will the Kuaha share the bounty of the Truth Stream with the people of the Undercity if we save them from their underground hell?'

'Son, why do you continue to oppose the humans? Why have you lost faith? You should be focused on what is best for the Truth Stream. The humans have been tending to the land with care. Even those trapped in the Undercity now strive to understand the meaning of love.'

'Please, Sansvira, pull me into your rock-face to dwell with you. Loneliness has blighted my wings. My heart aches for your company. Even if we repel the Aliens from our world, I will still be alone. Our Race will be lost, our language forgotten.'

'Epic, we are not immortal. We too have a limited life-span, an ending. Look more closely at us. Can you not feel our desire to be free again, to populate the Truth Stream? The time is near when things that seem impossible may become possible.'

Epic skipped back a pace as one of the Sansvira's wings broke free of the wall to touch his own. His eyes opened wide in astonishment.

'We must depart, dear one,' the Sansvira called. 'This effort is telling on our life force. Bless your endeavours. Life is mysterious and no one being has all the answers. Epic, travel with the humans. Help them. You will find companionship for now with those that cherish you. Otahi, Nua, Solo and the Ahorangi all work for the same goal as Powerflower, Keywee and ourselves – an enlightened world, one of peace and prosperity, kindness and love. We are glad you have seen into the rock and it is rewarding to touch you once more.'

'Epic,' Powerflower enthused, 'you see, there is a future.'

'Yes. Without your commitment, I would be stranded, caught inside my own unworthy trap. I feel ready now to fight again for the Truth Stream. Goodbye for now, Sansvira. When next you see me, you shall be released. Free again. We will all regain our rightful place in the Truth Stream.'

The Sansvira faded into the cliff-face, leaving Epic, Powerflower and Keywee shining with their own luminosity, lighting up the dell like heavenly bodies tracking each other's orbits.

'You have extraordinary powers, Epic – the ability to expand and retract – and since Neke bit you and saved your life, the fabulous talent of melding into your environment, becoming invisible. Use these advantages well. Oak's children are multiplying in Lair City, undetected as yet. They are converting the carbon dioxide back to oxygen, so it is safe on the fringes. Thanks to you, they are winning the battle, strangling the daughters of the Alien tree. But their subversion will be discovered sooner or later. You must convince Chief Otahi to act now. Rally his people. Keywee and I will work towards the same end.'

'Epic, the battle cannot be won without faith. We have watched Solo, too, struggling in the same dark corners of his soul. You are not alone in this.'

'I struggle no more, dear friends. I understand now that it is not what the world is that counts; it is what you make of the world. Let's make the Truth Stream healthy and whole again, and release the Sansvira, my tribe, the Superbird Race, and give humanity the chance to dwell in harmony with us.'

Mt Cloudcatcher in the Truth Stream

Chapter Eight

'For God's sake, Toby, get with the plan. The real world. Day and night you're writing this fantasy rubbish that no one cares about. Impossible worlds filled with violence and sick creatures. I know it's been hard for you, coming to terms with your father leaving us, but he was lazy and he spent all our money down at the pub. He preferred to be with his friends, not his family.

'I understand your need for escape, that's why I've let you closet yourself away, but now it's an obsession that has to stop. Find a job, help pay for the running of the house. You're 25 years old.

'Dammit, stop writing and listen to me. Your stepfather is angry. He's had enough. He'll throw you out onto the street. He's sick to death of your petulant behaviour. Christ, stop that and look at me! Do you hear me? You're a disaster. God, let some air and light in here. You're disgusting. This room stinks. Your stepfather will be home soon. He expects you to have dinner with us, do the dishes, and watch the rugby with him. His friends call you a faggot, a mummy's boy. It's embarrassing for him. His mates down at the meat-works are giving him a hard time.

'Jeez, how did I manage to end up with a son like you? I'm warning you! I won't stop Phil from clipping you around the ears and kicking your arse. For god's sake, you've been in here for two years, writing this drivel. No-one will ever read it! Toby, if you don't buck up your ideas, I'll kick you out myself. Why can't you be normal, happy in your skin?

'Phil's a good man. We'd be up shit-creek without him. His patience has run out. You're a rotten little brat. Grow up.

'Toby, look at this room. It's a tip. There's paper everywhere, on the floor, on your bed, your clothes are covered in ink, your sheets, even the carpet. You trash everything. Just because we don't read the nonsense that you write, there's no need to take it out on us.'

'Toby, don't you slap at my hand or swear at me. You wait until Phil gets home. God, you're in for it.'

'Well, leave the curtains alone, Mum, and don't slam the door when you go. I've nearly finished my book, and then I won't be troubling you any more. I'll move out. My book's not a fantasy, you know. It's the world I live in, and Phil is a character in it. A Lair. A programmed machine.'

'Don't call your stepfather a liar.'

'I didn't say liar. I said he's a Lair.'

'I've had it up to here with you, Toby. I tell you, your life changes or out you go. I don't give a damn if you have to live on the street.'

'Yes Mum, yes. Now please, I've got this book to finish. It's hard enough as it is without all your drama.'

'Drama! Drama!'

'Calm down, Ma, it's just an expression.'

'I'll give you drama.'

'Please, Mum, don't do that. No, Ma, no, no. That's an important section. I could kick you. You just deleted a week's work.'

'That's not work. Work is what your stepfather does. Work is what I do, washing, cleaning, cooking, getting your sister off to school, that's work. Tomorrow, you will go with Phil down to the abattoir and you will start a job. A good job that he's found for you packing meat. All this bullshit has to stop.

'Son, I love you. It's destroying me to watch you fritter away your life like this, locked up in your room. Phil will help you into the real world. I know you're scared of it. Phil could love you too, if you gave him a chance. He wants to. Perhaps the army would be a good idea. Make a man out of you. Look at Curly Simpson down the road. Look at what it's done for him. He's been around the world already.'

'Yeah, he's in Iraq, killing babies, Mum. Working for evil and its…'

'Stop it. At least he's a man, not a sissy like you.'

'I'm a sissy because I don't want to kill people? Rob people, rape people? Hello! My book reflects the real world and you call it garbage.'

'I've had enough. You've grown too big for your britches, Sonny Boy.'

'Don't you want to know how my book ends, Ma?'

'Ends? We couldn't even get through the first chapter, you silly boy. Do I have to spell it out to you? Your book is T.R.A.S.H. And all our friends think the same. Incomprehensible trash. Why, even your Uncle Bob couldn't and wouldn't read it. He said you can't even spell, for godsake, and that he wouldn't waste his time with such drivel.'

'Ha ha, good old Uncle Bob, the arbiter of taste, who thinks that wealth makes him knowledgeable, beyond reproach. Mum, he's not listening to you when you talk to him. He's too busy stroking his own ego, building a world of self-indulgence. It's all about Bob. Wake up, Mum, its all about his timetable. If you fit in with it, then he'll charm the pants off you. He's always selling something, usually himself.'

'That's it, Toby. Now you've gone too far. Your Uncle Bob has supported us for a long, long time. Before Phil. Before your father deserted us.'

'Mum, Uncle Bob's a bloody liar. Come on, Mum, you know it's true. He hides behind his money and power. Please, just let me finish my story. It's important to me! Doesn't that matter? Can't you cut me some slack? I've nearly finished. Then I'll get a real job, as you call it.'

'It's too late, Toby, You're a bad apple and you've hurt us all. You're selfish. You do know that, don't you? Look at all those library books, they're months overdue.'

'They're reference books. I need them for my work. I'll return them.'

'Crap. You're too lazy to return them. That's why they're still here.'

'Mum, this is doing neither of us any good.'

'Toby, I can't show my face down the club without being prodded and poked by my girlfriends. How's Shakespeare? they giggle. I'm the laughing stock. The butt of their jokes. All because of you and your stupid idea of writing a book. At first they had sympathy for you, now they believe it's a cover. That you're a nancy boy. Why, you won't even acknowledge them or leave your room when they come to visit. You have no friends. You're invited nowhere and you're a bad influence on your sister. I won't have her coming in here any more.'

'She comes to hear more of the story. She loves it. She asks for more, pleads. She's the only one who appreciates what I'm doing.'

'She's too young to know anything. And your story gives her nightmares. She wakes up crying.'

'It's you and Phil that give her nightmares with your drinking and arguing. Your fights, not my story. But you wouldn't know because you're too drunk to realise.'

'Oh God, how did I get such an awful son? You're just like your father. No good.'

'Then I'll move in with him. That should satisfy you and Phil. Just tell me how I can find him.'

'He's gone. Good riddance to bad rubbish. No-one knows where he is.'

'That's right Mum, no-one knows. Please don't slam the door. Ma…!

* * * * * * *

'Hi Betty, how was school?'

'It was okay. Don't listen to Mum, Toby. I think your story is cool. I heard her screaming at you. She's in the kitchen fuming, pouring herself another drink. She told me I wasn't allowed in here any more.'

'I know. I give you nightmares.'

'Well, your story is scary, but it doesn't give me nightmares. I cry because of them, Mum and Phil. I hate it when they go on benders and lose it, that's all. I cry because they're cruel to each other, but I never tell them that. I just say I had a nightmare. It's easier that way. Anyhow, I've sneaked in here, so we'll have to be quiet. Can I read more of the story? I'm up to where Zebu Manci is about to burn the Truth Stream. You're not going to let him, are you? The Kuaha will stop him, won't they? Superbird will save the earth, won't he?'

'I'd love to give it to you to read, but Mum's wiped the whole of that chapter from my computer, so I'll have to do it again. She's such a bitch.'

'Don't say that, Toby. It's Phil. He's putting her under so much pressure. Mummy loves you.'

'Sure, Betty, sure she does.'

'I'd better go, Toby. If Mum finds me in here, there'll be hell to pay. I hope you can finish your book.'

'Betty, I think things will be bad tonight. You should go out to your girlfriend's. Tell them it's to do homework. That'll please them.'

'Oh Toby, don't get into a fight with Phil. He has such a bad temper. I'm scared he'll hurt you.'

'I'll be okay, Betty. Go on, off you go.'

Chapter Nine

'A mouth full of clever words. You're cunning and clever. How is it you never ask after me? Yes, oh, oh, yes. More clever deceptions. Supply? Yes, without you I'd be licking on corpses, sure, but I wouldn't have to lend my ear to your carping. You know you do go on and on and on! Big deal, you're the witch's britches, important, the big noise, the big deal. So what? So am I. So there's no need to try to impale me on your spikes. So your daughters are struggling? So am I. Snake's blood. That's what I want. Go on, stuff yourself on this latest offering. More than you can digest. Look at you. Farting, belching. Letting go of your disgusting gasses. Putrid. Change your diet. Try some of those that feed you such shit. You have no idea. You sit here and get fat on fat! That's creepy. You want to try moving around. Around! you scream. Piss on you. So what if you've seen the universe, sunk your roots into many a planet. Puke! You're still just a tool of the Jaars. Without them you're nothing. Nothing, I tell you. Mancirians are more resilient, more capable. Hey, it's just a conversation. Wooo, yes, yes, okay, I'll get to work. Here, move that branch closer. It's covered in juicy ticks. Stop that, I'm not edible. My skinny body wouldn't feed a twig of one of your daughters.

'Look, there goes Zebu Manci with his pet Dr Steel. That's who rules this city, not the Jaars. Especially not Laxman. Oh, shitty thorns, here he comes, to bang his head against your trunk again I suppose. Wish I didn't have to listen to his drivel.'

'Acheron Afrit, I hope you're satisfied. I will offer you the Mancirian Zebu before too long. He will be a meal in himself. Something truly full of fat. He has deluded himself beyond his station. Jaars shall rule this planet. Give me the strength, blessed tree, to bring him as an offering to your scarlet trunk.'

Chapter Ten

'Jeez, Bob, don't do that. If Phil catches you he'll rip your balls out. Stop it, Bob.'

'Come on, Lesley, you love it.'

'Shit, Phil's in the lounge. You're not here to fool around. You're here to straighten out Toby.'

'Bugger the little shit. He's beyond help, upstart know-all prick.'

'Bob, get your hands out of there. Bob! Christ, Bob, just take the chips and dip into the lounge. Before Phil comes searching for us.'

Uncle Bob, dear old Uncle Bob. Fresh from his office, staff drinks, tie hanging loosely around his neck, shirt sleeves rolled to his elbows. He checks his watch, then plods across the lino, his hairy hands clutching two bowls, and collides with Phil's beer-pot, which moves in front of him, blocking Bob's progress.

'Hell, Bob, the game's about to start. Come on mate. Don't want to miss kick-off. Lesley, bring us a few more beers, hon.' The words slur from under Phil's walrus moustache, his thin upper lip hidden. He's in a singlet, his thick arms encircled by tattoos. Barbed-wire coils snake down their length, finishing on the backs of his hands.

For a moment he stares over Bob's shoulder and squints one eye in Lesley's direction before turning on his fence-post legs to follow Bob into the lounge and the sound of a blaring voice predicting a tight struggle between the two arch-rivals. 'What a game we have for you tonight,' the commentator declares.

'How's that receptionist you got down there? Now, she's cute. I'd love to give her one. What do ya reckon, Bob, any chance?'

Bob laughs. 'Shit, Phil, have you seen yourself in the mirror lately? Fat bloody chance, mate.'

Phil giggles. 'She's got great tits.'

'Forget it, Phil.'

Lesley comes in, bottles clinking. She leans over to place them on the side table. Her skirt drifts up as she bends.

'God, you got a fab arse love,' Phil screams, 'but it's covering the telly, so move, will ya?'

Bob pats the sofa next to him. 'Come and sit here, darl,' he chirps. Phil belches and grabs a handful of crisps, stuffing them past his whiskers while lifting his bottle to his mouth. Lesley eyes both men.

'You're bloody pigs. I've got baking to do. Can't you turn it down a bit Phil, it's friggen loud.'

'Piss off, it's Friday footy.'

'Listen, Phil, Bob's here to talk to Toby, remember? So don't get too reved up, ok?'

'Yeah, okay. After the game, love. Little shit, should be watching it with us. Bet he's in there playing with himself. He's queer, that kid. We'll go and spring him at half-time. That'll be a laugh, eh, Bob?'

'How's it down at the works?' Bob asks.

'Oh, much the same. Looks like a short season again. Dollar's working against us. No money in exporting so the farmers are hanging on to their stock.'

'Still flogging boxes of fillet, are you?'

'You bet, mate. You want some? Ten bucks a fillet. A bloke's got to survive. Fuck 'em. They can afford it. Rotten multi-nationals.'

'Hell, Phil, you've got some cheek. You wouldn't last a minute in my company.'

'Well, you want some or not?'

'Yeah, sure, I'll have a couple.'

'You're a hypocrite, Bob.'

'Well, it's no skin off my nose. How's your beer? Want another?'

The empties stack up, the men cheer their team on, screaming obscenities at the ref and linesmen, bemoaning decisions that ultimately cause the defeat of their team. Phil's livid. Bob's disappointed in their new first-five.

'Jeez, Phil, you could have played a better game. That damned coach couldn't find a beer in a brewery. Useless bastard. He's got to go.'

'You're not wrong, mate.'

Both men are drunk now, loud, and obnoxious. Phil pulls himself up out of his recliner chair. The footrest slides back under the armchair with a bang. He stamps over to the TV, slaps the off button and lurches towards the liquor cabinet for something stronger.

'Want a whiskey?' he asks Bob.

'Why not? Might as well drown our sorrows. We'll need it to get through to Toby, anyhow. Go get the little shit, Phil. I've got a squeeze to punish. Told her I'd be over after the game.'

'Jeez, don't know how you get away with it. Doesn't Gloria suspect?'

'Na, I'll just tell her it took more time to sort out Toby than I'd expected.'

'Shit, Bob, don't know how ya do it. Gloria's a doll.'

'Mate! We're both lucky guys. Your Lesley's one too. Come on, get Toby and let's get it over with.'

Phil puts his arm around Bob. Bob feels Phil's strength as he tightens his grip. 'You're a good bloke. Thanks for this. I know Lesley thinks you're part of the family and she's so relieved you're here. I know you're a busy bastard, got a lot on…'

'Look at you two,' Lesley squawks as she stumbles into the lounge. She's been baking alright, baking her brain while chatting on the phone. She's holding a glass and the ice cubes bounce together, playing out a brittle tune.

'I'll get Toby,' Phil says, and strides down the dingy hallway to the bedroom door. He's feeling mean and he's going to sort Toby out, once and for all.

Bob grabs at Lesley's ample breasts and pushes them together, lunging at her neck like a vampire.

'God, Bob, I like that,' she whispers in his ear. They tear themselves apart as all hell breaks loose. They can hear Phil's voice at full throttle, bodies banging against the plaster walls and Toby screaming at Phil to take his hands off him.

Lesley races out of the room, frightened by Phil's temper, alarmed to see him dragging her son toward her.

'Let him go, Phil. Phil!'

Bob's there too now, calming Phil down, separating his claws from Toby. The bedroom door hangs off one hinge.

'Come on Phil, quieten down, mate.'

'I'll teach him who's in charge around here. Little prick. Called me an arsehole. I'll give him arsehole.'

Lesley tries to help Toby to his feet. Toby's having none of it and repels her assistance.

'Come, on Toby,' Bob coos. 'Take it easy, son. Your parents just want to help you. You don't know how much they care. They're worried, that's all. Now let's go into the kitchen and talk, like grown ups. It's the least you can do.'

Bob moves in behind Toby and puts his arm around his shoulder. The hallway's crowded. They're all pressed together. Toby turns his face to the wall, trying to escape the heavy odour of alcohol that lingers on their breath.

'Go on, you two,' Bob says. 'Toby and I will be in. Give us a moment, okay?'

Phil's face is red with rage. Spittle flies from his mouth as he is led back down the hallway by Lesley whose dream of a quiet conversation is shattered. She's shaking but still has hold of her glass.

'Now, you shut up Phil and let Bob do the talking,' she says, as they disappear into the kitchen.

'What do you care, Bob? Shouldn't you be out fucking somebody over, stealing their hard-earned cash?' Toby says to Bob.

'Look, I'm not really going to put up with this shit from you. I'm doing this for your mum. Now you can either do this the easy way, or the hard way. That's up to you.'

'Well, Bob, we'd better get it over with then,' Toby replies.

The kitchen lights illuminate each chair. Lesley and Phil sit opposite each other, silent. Phil's twiddling his thumbs, biting his bottom lip while he taps the formica table top. Lesley stares into the dregs of her drink as Bob sits Toby down and reaches for the last chair. Scraping its legs across the floor, he plonks himself down. Lesley's hand shoots out and covers Phil's. She smiles at him. Phil lifts his eyelids and returns a weak sneer. His legs are moving under the table doing an impatient jig. Bob stretches his neck and pulls his tie back into place, unrolls his cuffs and buttons them. Brushing down his shirt with his hands, he leans back in his chair and places his locked fingers behind his head.

'Now, Toby, your folks have asked me to come over and explain a few facts of life to you.'

Toby's eyes are glued to the table top. He's thinking how easily Phil could be converted into a Lair, and how simple it would be to make Bob a Mancirian – an alien despot.

'I'll make some coffee,' Lesley offers, and turns towards Phil as she stands, one finger up to her lips, making a pleading gesture for him to behave.

'Now, Toby,' Bob says, 'what are you going to do with your life?'

'Write books, Bob. Why? What are you going to do with yours? Strip people of their assets, fuck your mate's wives? Destroy the environment?'

'You little bastard,' Phil screams.

Bob grabs Phil halfway across the table. Lesley starts to cry, dropping a coffee cup. It shatters on the lino.

'Listen Toby, your attitude's not going to make you friends and friends are what you need in this life, if you want to get ahead.'

'Shit, Bob, why don't you become my friend and tell me how much you admire my aptitude and commitment to writing?'

'That trash you turn out isn't writing, Toby. Sheldon, Clavell... the woman who wrote *Valley of the Dolls*. What's her name? That's writing.'

'Joan Collins,' Lesley says through her sobs.

'You can't even spell, Toby. You're not clever enough, son. I've tried to read your book. I only managed a couple of pages. It doesn't take a genius to know you haven't got it. Your book's full of impossible characters, improbable places. And those silly pictures that you draw. I'm sorry, Toby, to tell you the truth. I'm not trying to hurt you, mate, but it's over. I've met some writers. Met Barry Crump once. Now there was a writer. A good bloke. Great to have a beer with. He had friends. Lots of them.'

'Oh Christ, Bob, let's forget this. He's not even listening to you,' Phil screams at the light bulb, stamping his feet under the table. 'He has to go. I want him out of this house. Selfish little shit.'

'Did you hear that, Toby?' Bob says through his clenched teeth. 'Phil wants you out. And to be frank with you, I understand his frustration.'

'Phil's a cock-sucker like you are Bob. Full of yourselves, incapable of opening your minds to anything different.'

'That's it, you little arsehole,' Phil yells, tipping the table in his booze-heightened hatred of his stepson, leaving Bob marooned in his chair, arms held above his head protecting himself from the table as it smashes into the kitchen wall. Toby's on the floor, also sliding into the wall, while Lesley's in shock, looking down at her leg which has a deep gash, spilling blood liberally onto her favourite shoes.

'Fuck you, I'm going to kill you, you dumb-head,' Phil roars as he pounds Toby. The sound of his fists smacking into Toby's face fills the room. Bob's now on his feet. He's ashen-faced. This is too much even for him. 'Shit, Phil, stop it. You'll kill him for sure.'

He's grappling with Phil's arms, trying to hold Phil in a bear hug. Phil's kicking Toby in the stomach, arms, anywhere he can land a decent blow. Toby's in a foetal position, silently waiting for the attack to stop.

'Phil, Phil, Phil! Lesley's hurt, mate. Christ, stop, mate,' Bob screams at Phil. 'Lesley, mate. She's bleeding.'

'Come on, Bob, help me throw him out. He's garbage and garbage belongs in the street.'

Phil exhausts his barrage. His clenched knuckles are skinned, his T-shirt speckled with dark stains. He's breathing hard through his nose, glaring down at Toby. At last Bob is able to pull him a few steps back. Bob's words register in Phil's thick skull. He turns to look at Lesley. She lies slumped to the floor against the sink cupboard. 'You bastard,' Phil screams. 'Look what you've done to your mother,' and he turns back to Toby, pulls him up by his hair and drags him to the front door. Ripping it open, he flings Toby down the concrete steps. He hears the air explode from Toby's lungs, and then slams the door shut, yelling at him to fuck off and not come back. Then he runs back to find Bob on his haunches, stroking Lesley's hair and asking her if she's alright.

'Oh hell, here, let me have a look. You'll be okay. It's not that deep, sweetie. I'll fix it. I'll fix it,' Phil says.

* * * * * * *

Toby's body aches in places he never knew existed. He has pulled himself up onto the small patch of lawn that separates the house from the footpath. He's gasping for air and trying to sit upright. He keeps falling back onto his side. Small animal moans escape his mouth.

This is how Betty finds him, on her way home from her girlfriend's.

'Toby. No! Oh, Toby. I told you not to rile Phil up. God Toby,' she squeals, bending over to look into his puffy, bruised eyes. Blood seeps from his lower lip. Toby tries to laugh, but it hurts and he starts to cough.

'I'm okay, Betty. I wanted to leave anyway,' he whispers.

'No, you're not alright.'

'Betty, Betty, please go and get my laptop. Please Betty. That's all I need. Get it now, before Phil smashes it. Please Betty. It has my book in it. Run, Betty. Hurry.'

Betty drops her things by his side. She looks at her brother, who is trying once again to sit upright, propping himself by his one good arm.

'Hurry, Betty.'

She's afraid, as she gently opens the front door and peers down the hall. She can hear Bob and Phil in the kitchen and like a mouse she moves towards Toby's room, looking back over her small shoulder. She runs to the laptop, unplugs it, grabs the disks piled beside it and tippy-toes back to the door and out onto the lawn.

'Here,' she says, 'Phil's a pig for doing this to you.'

'Thanks, Betty. You're the best sister a brother can have.'

'Where will you go, Toby? Here's my pocket-money.'

'Don't worry, little Betty. I'll be fine. I don't need your money, I've got some. You'd better get inside before Phil comes out again. Go on. Please, Betty.'

Toby watches her slide inside. Her innocent face peeks back at him and blows a kiss before she disappears.

'Bye, Betty,' he says to himself. 'Bye sis. Love you, Betty.'

Chapter Eleven

'Let's sit on the veranda. We'll be more comfortable,' the Ahorangi says. 'My old bones could use some sun. It's a bit chilly in the Meeting House.'

He leads me to a bench, then chuckles. 'Looks like we won't be sunning ourselves after all.' He is right, as he is in most things. No sooner have we sat down than the sun vanishes behind a massive band of thick black sooty cloud in the west. 'The edge of the Truth Stream is ablaze. The trees call out for help. The wild-life is in a panic, confused, lost in the flames and smoke.'

'I know,' I reply meekly.

'Otahi has sent a small force to combat the Alien's progress, forcing them back across the Great River.'

'Yes, I know,' I repeat.

'The woman Silk slumbers in Oak's roots in the Undercity. She has visited me in my dreams. She has told me that Neke now dwells, hidden, within the Alien's likeness, surviving on the tiniest amount of oxygen that Oak pumps to her from Silk's room. It is a miracle Oak lives, and she is holding back from sprouting limbs.'

'I envy you your time with Silk. I long for her to touch my dreams once more.'

'She will Solo, when the time is right. For now, be happy that Keywee graced you with her presence. Otherwise you would be encased in a block of ice on Mt Cloudcatcher. Solo, Otahi has asked me to tell you to find Nua. Bring him home. We attack Lair City. He is needed.'

'How is that possible? I've tried for two moons to find him. I thought it would be easy. Now I wouldn't know where to start.'

'Just follow the wood pigeons. They will lead you to him.'

'Wood Pigeons?' I ask.

'Yes. Since he was a young child, they have always kept him company. His parents, if they were ever in need of him, just followed the flight of one and headed in that direction. It never failed. He was always somewhere close by.'

Suddenly, my head feels like the brooding cloud brewing above us, gobbling up what little blue sky there is.

'Why have you not told me of this before?'

'You never asked, Solo.'

'What if he won't come?'

'He will come. He has to. He has no choice. Nua knows this.'

A light rain begins to fall. The dry dusty compound comes to life and in the distance, lightning flashes, slicing the sky apart. The Enlightened One looks at me and smiles. 'Seems the heavens have answered our call. The Truth Stream fights back. Our warriors will have no problem repelling the Lairs. They will flee back into Lair City. The fires will be doused. See, we do not work alone to reclaim what is ours.'

'Does nothing unravel you, Ahorangi?'

'There is nothing I can do that is not already being done, Solo.'

'There is one thing, Ahorangi. Nua's hatred of Jall will not have ceased.'

'Then there is good reason for this, and I will advise Otahi to keep Jall from our war plans.'

'May I tell Nua this?'

'Yes, of course, Solo.'

'It will be hard to find a pigeon about in this weather,' I say as the rain increases, falling in heavy sheets that blanket the village. The silhouetted trees and hills, like cut-outs, recede into the rising mist.

The Enlightened One stands, then steps into the torrent. 'I don't think so,' he says. 'If I am out in it, then I'm sure a pigeon will be.' And he pulls the staff he has been leaning on into the air and moves it in an arc across the watery terrain, stopping on a dull speck that moves towards us from the east. His staff tracks its progress, and it increases in size until, finally, I know what it is.

The pigeon labours past, only a matter of feet above his head, battling the downpour, turning towards the west, low to the ground, across the gardens. It disappears somewhere near a trail I have walked many times. The Enlightened One then returns, dripping wet, to the cover of the veranda. He smiles again.

'It will be waiting for you, in the trees with others, I suspect.

Remember they are quiet birds, silent when at rest. They will be hidden, but look amongst the foliage for their white chest patches. I sense Nua is not that far away. Closer than one might think.'

I look closely into his face. His eyes sparkle in the gloom as he pats me on the shoulder.

'I believe I will see you and Nua before this day ends. I will wait inside the Meeting House with Otahi. I know Nua will wish to come in under the cover of night. He will want his home-coming to go undetected. A matter only between his chief and the two of us.'

'I will go and pack a few supplies and be on my way, then.'

'You won't need supplies, Solo. Just your coat to keep the rain from your skin,' he says, moving back to the bench. A pool of water collects around his bare feet. He stares into the angry heavens that clap with thunder, followed closely by lightning, illuminating his diminutive body. He clutches his staff in front of him. With each clash of thunder he laughs, roaring out his approval.

I can still hear him as I trot from the village along the flight path of the bird, and for the briefest moment, I think it is the Ahorangi's laughter that brings forth such clatter and the fierce display of jagged bolts of light that rip apart the sky. Vulnerable in the open field, I quicken my pace, speeding towards the safety of the canopy. Mud splashes onto all parts of my body. My trousers are heavy, caked with the stuff. I am saturated and as soon as I stop running, I realise how cold I am.

I shiver while sheltering under a puriri tree, questioning the Ahorangi's wisdom about needing supplies. I am in a quandary. Should I return for more protection? After all, how long can this rain fall for? Then another almighty flash above my head. I look up at the brilliant display. It lights up the tree and dotted throughout its branches are dozens of wood pigeons, all with their heads bowed, looking directly at me. They drop, one after the other, from its boughs, looping in graceful swoops, like ghostly kites dipping away from the track and deeper into the forest. From tree to tree they glide, unhindered by the turmoil and murderous banging storm that pelts all it has at the land.

Some wait while I clamber over small rocky hillocks. I knock my shins and elbows in the pursuit. The sound of the pigeons' wings competes with the thunder claps. Their majestic bodies are cloaked in muted grey and bruised violet feathers, and are lost to sight at times against the brooding sky.

They lead me forward, diving in curved arcs, and finally into a dell which is ringed by sharp pointed cliffs. To one side, an overhanging ledge protects a cave that has smoke seeping from its entrance. I rush into its mouth, calling Nua's name.

Startled, he jumps up from the fire, holding out his club. Then, just as quickly, drops it to his side. Solo,' he yells. 'How I've longed to see you.'

'It is the same for me,' I manage to squirt out from between my frozen lips, making for the warmth of his fire.

'Get your clothes off,' he says while adding more fuel to the licking flames. He places his tattered feathered cloak across my shoulders. My body tingles back to life as my clothes are laid out on rocks to dry.

'How did you find me in such weather, my friend?'

'Wwwooodddd ppppiggeooons,' I stammer, rubbing at the frozen parts of my body. 'Thththe Enlllightteeened Ooonne tttold mmmee.'

'Here, eat this,' he says. 'It will warm you.' And he places some eel in my shaking fingers.

The food and the cosy care soon have their effect. Nua piles more wood on. The fire crackles, flicking our shadows around the walls.

'Yes, the pigeons have always been interested in my company. Perhaps it's because I have always protected them. Never taken any for my plate or cloak. Whatever the reason, I'm glad they have led you to me. In ancient times they were called kukupa, kereru, kuku, but they are just as happy with wood pigeon.'

Moving back from the heat, thawed at last, I watch my clothes drying. Plumes of vapour escape the cavern into the violent storm.

'I've come to collect you. Chief Otahi demands your presence, your counsel. We move against the Aliens and Lair City.'

'Impossible!' Nua bellows. 'As long as the white devil Jall is close to my brother, I cannot return.'

Nua is on his feet, prowling the cave. His shadowed figure dances in animated gestures like a wild man. 'Never!' he roars again.

How deeply embedded is his hate for Jall. I, too, make it to my feet and grab hold of him. 'Nua, listen. The Ahorangi told me to tell you Jall will not be privy to our plans. He knew you would not come if Jall was invited into the Meeting House. The Enlightened One now waits for you.'

Nua's mad movements stops, his shoulders relax. He takes a deep breath and his eyes pierce mine.

'Ahh, Solo, brother. I trust you and you alone, to tell this news. Please, let's sit a while. I know it shocks you to see me like this, bent out of shape.'

As his rage subsides, so does the chaotic tempest outside. The onslaught is abating, calming like Nua's mood.

'Solo, two days ago I was near the Great River. I had seen smoke billowing above it, so I went to find its source. I saw many Lairs hacking into our trees, burning them alive, and my eyes were hurting, my soul was stripped from my being. I knew our warriors would soon arrive to kill the Lairs and put a stop to this affront, and I was just about to move out when, to my astonishment, Jall appeared just a few feet from me on the track, heading for the bridge. He walked straight through the hoards of Lairs, holding something out. What, I do not know. The Lairs followed him and then I saw he was heading for the most hideous of creatures that one could ever dream of. Aliens. A massive beast towered over Jall and he talked with Jall for some time. Alone. Then let him go. Let him go!

'Jall raced back up the track. I stalked him. I was going to finish his miserable life and leave him to be discovered close to the village. I missed my chance. All too soon he was met by Kuaha warriors and slipped away from my club.'

I sit, transfixed by Nua's story, entranced, struggling with his words. Straining to understand, wrestling with Nua's tale, I am stupefied at the lengths to which he will go to denounce Jall.

He must see the dilemma on my face, for he says, 'You don't believe me, do you Solo? I trusted that you of all people would.'

I feel shame. I look away. 'Allow me a moment, Nua, to digest your words. I do not care for Jall, but your story is fantastic. Almost unbelievable. Scary to think about. I'm trying to envisage such a meeting. You know, he came back to the village surrounded by men extolling him as a hero. His mana is huge. He claimed to have been scouting, searching like you for the source of the burning.'

Nua says nothing as I stumble along with my thoughts.

'You cannot tell any other of this, dear friend. It will be taken badly at the village. Some would say boils have swamped your heart.'

Nua's dejected face seems snagged, hooked by fate. Deep shadows cut across his tattooed face, his hands caress his club. He is a man alone. A Kuaha warrior, the brother of the Paramount Chief, who has placed himself in exile rather than bring shame to his family. And here am I, wearing his cloak, a prized possession, and questioning his mana, his word. How do I manage to doubt this man? What is wrong with me? Then I realise, with the sudden force of an axe against a tree, that I am afraid of conflict. I want to sit on the fence. I have pushed my head into a hole. I am running away from my destiny, scared to take a stand. Weary of disputes. I should never have questioned Nua's truths. He would never question mine.

'Jall must die!" I say.

Nua lifts his face from his club, and a crease ripples down his cheeks to catch his lips, curling them into the biggest smile I have ever seen. I return his cloak and step into my dry clothes with clarity in my veins.

'If my brother calls, then I must go,' Nua says. 'To him we give our lives and take those that would threaten his.'

Through Nua's stealth, we make it to the Meeting House unseen. Chief Otahi and the Enlightened One are waiting, just as he promised. The Chief's eyes are glassy with tears of joy at the sight of his brother's return. A tinge of blue can be seen emanating from behind the centre pole and another in the rafters. And out of the corner of my eye, I realise there is a pale green light humming behind us. A great gathering is taking place. It burrows into my scalp. I shudder at its importance. A moment in the history of man is about to unfold. The air holds a tension that elevates me beyond my normal self. The power in this house is extraordinary; it's filled with a current so forceful I almost lose my balance. A potent well of knowledge is about to be unleashed.

Nua walks up to his brother and presses his nose against that of his Chief. Then he bows to the Ahorangi. I follow behind, slip-streaming in his wake. Now we are a tight group in the middle of the House, fizzing with feelings of love and hope, waiting for the lights to join us.

Keywee, streamlined, clad in a skilfully polished coat, is first to our side, followed by Powerflower's adroit petals, translucent, clipping and weaving, hovering close to my grinning face. Then Epic springs from behind the centre pole, a commanding entrance that holds the attention of us all. He strides like a colossus across the matted floor, wings wide apart to gather us into his expanding embrace, cocooning us tent-like, as one. His head is like a roof that we all look up to, his eyes blazing, hypnotic.

There is something about his energy that is new, or have I missed it on other occasions? He seems more solid, more attached to himself, less ethereal. Happy, in a way I find difficult to explain.

I notice the Ahorangi stroking his chin, deep in thought, also trying to get a handle on the Superbird. Epic winks at him, directly at him. The Enlightened One lets out a 'wooo' as if he understands. Keywee folds herself at our feet and tips back her trumpet beak and kawaddles, a soft sound that massages our very skin and bones, while Powerflower's petals brush across our jubilant faces. I feel as if all the horrific battles I have ever witnessed have been cast away and replaced with visions of a peaceful Truth Stream.

Then Powerflower condenses to the size of a hand, floating above Keywee's sleek body. All of us are wrapped in the vibrations, somehow both comforting and thrilling, that shoot from Epic's wings. We sway gently together.

Otahi announces, 'It is time. Time to free our world from the Aliens. Time to take back the Truth Stream. For we are the Gatekeepers. This night will be recorded on our walls. Even the heavens agree, banishing the Lairs back to their putrid city, extinguishing their fires, reclaiming our lands.'

Then Nua speaks. 'Jall is a traitor, brother. It has to be said. A planted creature of the Alien's will. He shares their ambitions, fraternises with them. I have seen it. I have to warn you. He is not what he seems.'

I think a boulder is about to fall and squash us all. I wait for Chief Otahi to fling Nua from our circle. Yet it does not come. Otahi just nods.

'Yes, you are right, dear brother, as Epic has confirmed, but he is useful for now. We will not change our approach to this evil dog. He will lead us to the Aliens. Then he will be dispatched like them.'

'How is it that Epic knows of Jall's sinister plans?' I ask, for I still have a lingering desire to give him the benefit of the doubt because he saved Chief Otahi's life.

'While you were away from the village Solo,' Epic said, 'I found him stealing Oak's acorns from your hut. He only took two handfuls, but I followed him into the forest. There he cracked them open, pulverising the seeds to dust. I returned to your dwelling and removed the rest. I hid them in the snail cages and I've been dropping them from the sky above the polluted atmosphere on the edges of the city.'

I feel myself shrinking inside. 'I have failed you,' I stammer. 'I have neglected my post as the keeper of Oak's acorns.'

'You weren't to know, Solo. I, too, have been fooled by Jall. Remember? We all have, except for Nua, who almost paid the ultimate price for his sanity. Jall has an agenda that none could possible have seen. He wants to rule the Truth Stream. The idiot thinks he can make a deal with the Aliens. It has always been his goal. His brain is crippled. He loves nothing. He's no more than a scheming weevil. A worm that thought he could deceive even the greater Universe. Who knows what evil intentions he entertains in his maggot mind.'

I feel dizzy, sick in my stomach. I want to lower myself to Nua's feet and ask for forgiveness, throw myself into the Great River and be carried away in its watery arms. I have been the weak link in this ring.

The Ahorangi leans into me. 'Solo, your part in this is ordained. You bless us with your presence.' He rubs my forehead then, and my thoughts are cleansed of my self-loathing. I take control of my body again, within the shelter of my friends' unconditional love.

'Tomorrow, we march for the Great River, then on to the Snail Cages. Epic has told me the area has been abandoned and is safe. It is there we will assemble. Ready ourselves for battle.'

'The fauna and flora are ready to march with you,' Powerflower intones.

'So too are the creatures that dwell in the Truth Stream,' Keywee trumpets.

'And I,' says Epic, 'will penetrate Lair City and contact Neke. Together, we will rally the Undercity folk and give them courage for their attack from below. The Oracle Silk is working there now, through Oak. Her strength and commitment are unshakeable. She reaches out even while we speak, gathering news of our approach. She has that ability. She will already be relaying this to her people.'

Keywee in the Truth Stream

Chapter Twelve

Toby rolls over onto all fours. He coughs a rattling laugh into the lawn. A mixture of pain and relief. A sweet and sour thrill. He had hated life under Phil's roof, hated that his mother chose to live with such a redneck bastard. How she changed, hardened, let herself go to seed. She cared for herself once, dressed smartly, was always bright and cheerful. Then his father left. Just got up and went, pretty much with nothing. Just walked through the door.

It's what he should have done, should have had the courage to do, instead of exiling himself in his room to write a book no-one cares for anyway. What if they're right? What if it is a piece of crap? Betty loves it, he reminds himself. He should have told her that she was Bella in his book, that he modelled Bella on her and Race on Sam, her best boyfriend, the one that was always running after her, carrying her books, laughing, saying, 'by jingoes, Betty, I like being with you.'

He lifts his head to see silhouetted figures behind the curtained kitchen. All arms and hands, moving erratically behind the screen like some Indonesian puppet play. The familiar characters, sliding to centre stage then flinging themselves to the wings. An ancient drama of greed and lust, fear and aggression. It could easily be the Lair City of his book. Phil looks the picture of a Lair, his big square head tipping back on his massive shoulders, screaming at Toby's mother, ready to pull her apart and drag her to some unknown hell.

Toby watches his mother with her hands to her face. He can tell she is crying. It rips at his heart. He licks at his stinging lip, tasting his own blood while lifting his laptop to get to his feet. Pain shoots through his body as he tucks the computer under his arm and limps away past identical houses with their identical patches of lawn, each locked down for the night.

Amputated plane trees line the street. Radically pruned, they stand ghost-like under the incandescent street lamps, sharing his injured progress through a star-filled night with a slipper moon balanced precariously in the sky, looking as though it might fall and break in pieces at his feet.

Each time a car rolls down the street he feels like a rabbit caught in its lights, spotted and ready to be shot. He hobbles on, clenching his teeth, trying to deal with his pain. He manages a few blocks to a quiet lane that ends near the beach. He thinks he might sleep there tonight, then shivers, thinking of the cold sand. Maybe a hedge would be better, or maybe climb under someone's house? Tears trickle down his face.

'Stop it,' he says aloud, sniffing back the gunk that blocks his nose. 'Stop it. Stop feeling sorry for yourself. Grow up, kid. No one cares,' he mumbles, exhausted, throbbing with pain from the bruises that cover his body and aching jaw.

He has to sit and take a rest. This is as good a place as any he thinks, slumping gingerly to the curb. Placing his laptop next to him, he checks his legs and arms, lifts his bloodied shirt, touches his ribs, impressed by the dark purple rings that circle the swollen bumps and welts. Blowing his nose into the gutter he wipes his hands on his pants.

He hears voices heading his way, down the lane. Laughter. It sounds like one guy and two girls. He wants to hide, goes to move, but his body complains. Resigned, he places his head between his knees, hoping they will pass on the other side, that they won't notice him, and if they do, that they'll leave him be. He can hear their footsteps getting closer, their voices whispering. Then a hand on his shoulder and a bloke's voice asking, 'Hey, man, you alright?'

'Yep, mate, yep,' he says through his thick lip.

'No, he's not,' one of the girl's voices says. 'He's been beaten up. Look at his shirt, his arms.'

'Hey, pal, can we get you a cab? Where do you live,' the bloke says, now on his haunches by Toby's side. The girls are standing over them, their hands to their mouths.

'Come on, mate, let's help you to your feet,' the bloke says, gently holding Toby's arm. Toby lets out an 'ouch' and lifts his head from between his knees to look at the bloke. The girls give out little cries, 'my god, who did this to you?'

'My stepfather,' Toby says weakly. 'He's thrown me out.'

'But why did he thrash you so bad. Your eyes are almost closed. Your lip looks like it might need a stitch or two. You don't look so good. Where are your bags?'

'I have none. All I managed to get is my computer. Well, actually, my little sister got it for me.'

'What? Have you got no clothes, nothing but your laptop?' one of the girls asks. 'It must mean something to you to only grab the computer, and nothing more.'

'It's got my novel in it. I've been working on it for three years. That's why he threw me out.'

'What? That's insane,' she says, then walks away, pulling the bloke and the other girl across the lane.

Toby can just make out the huddle they are in, just hear them talking to each other but not what is being said. The bloke comes back.

'Come to our place,' he says. 'Let's see if we can clean you up, give you a bed for the night. Work something out tomorrow. I'm sure your stepfather will be feeling sorry for himself and want you back home. Kate, hey Kate, get his laptop, will you?' the bloke says, grunting, as he tries to lift Toby. 'Shit, you're a heavy lad. Sharee, give us a hand, willya?'

Toby tries his best to help, but his body has seized, locked up tight. They live close by, only two houses down behind a large paling fence and a big sign in red letters, Guard Dogs, Keep Out. Toby couldn't care less. He has already been mauled.

'I'm not tucker for your dog,' he jokes as they bring him through the gate. All three of them laugh.

'Glad you've got a sense of humour, mate. My name's Ben, what's yours?'

'Toby,' he says, as they support him into their home.

Inside, in the light, they are even more shocked at Toby's state. 'Your stepfather's one hell of a fella,' Sharee says, easing him into an armchair.

'Yeah, a real man,' Toby manages to say.

'What about your Mum? Why does she let him treat you this way?'

Tears start to run down Toby's cheeks again.

'Let's not talk too much,' Kate says. 'I'll make some tea.'

'I think something stronger,' Ben suggests. 'Whiskey, Toby? What do you reckon, old mate?'

Toby nods, tries to smile, wiping at his tears with the crook of his arm.

'I'll go make up a bed for Toby,' Sharee announces.
'I'll help,' Kate says.

* * * * * * *

'Wow, Kate. Can you imagine what sort of animal would do that to a son?'

'Jeez, Sharee, imagine being married to it. What a life she must be having, seeing such things happening and not being able to do a thing.'

'Come on Kate, she could ring the cops, have him arrested, for godsake. Leave the bastard, surely, do something. It's her boy, after all. I suppose Toby could be telling us lies, spinning us a story? And maybe he was caught doing something bad, like stealing or… I don't know, something not right. I mean it's only his word that it's his laptop. Maybe it's…'

'Yeah, I thought of that. We'll move him out tomorrow. I'd prefer to believe he's telling the truth. He doesn't look like a thief. He's kind of cute. Well, you can see he might be good-looking when his wounds heal.'

'Oh Kate, you always see the good side of people. I love you for that.'

'I'm going to see if he would like a bath, soak his bones. Ask Ben if he would let him borrow a t-shirt and pair of jeans. You don't mind, do you Sharee, I'll wash his while he's in the bath. They can dry overnight.'

'Not at all. I'm sure Ben will only be too happy to let him have something to wear. They look pretty similar in size. I bet he could do with a feed as well. Let's believe he's the type who will appreciate our care.'

* * * * * * *

Back in the lounge Ben is sitting next to Toby, refilling his glass. Toby's lip is no longer seeping blood. It looks better, though more swollen, and doesn't seem to need stitches.

'I've run a bath for you, Toby. What do you say? Is it a good idea? Ben can help you into it. Will you Ben?' Kate asks.

'Sure, be just the cat's whiskers. Relax those muscles of yours.'

'Thanks, you guys,' Toby whispers. 'Thanks so much. It will be great to soak a while.'

Ben comes back with Toby's clothes. Kate stuffs them into the washing machine while Sharee and Ben discuss Toby's story. Kate returns to find them plugging in Toby's computer, Ben saying 'There's only one way to find out.'

They stand looking at the screen, waiting for it to confirm Toby's story. Ping, up it pops with the title page, *The Birth of Superbird*... And page after page of the typed story that Ben begins to read aloud.

'Wow, this is good. Awesome. Do you think we should tell him we've broken into his laptop? It's amazing he had no password protecting it. Must be a trusting sort of chap.'

'No,' Kate said. 'I think it's wrong of us, doing this. I wish we hadn't.'

'But at least we know he's telling us the truth, Kate. That makes us feel better, safer. We'll be able to sleep easy. I'll go and see if he needs help getting out of the bath,' Ben says, walking down the hallway.

'Tell him there's scrambled eggs waiting, will you love?' Sharee calls.

* * * * * * *

Toby wakes. He feels ill. One eye is fully closed, the other a slit he can just see through. His body feels smashed. He drags himself up to the headboard, moaning with the effort. He can smell coffee filtering under his door, into the room he's been sleeping in, which is filled with colourful paintings, stylised works. A clock by his bed shows 11am.

'Oh god,' he says to himself, as he squeezes out from under the coverings, holding onto the bed with both hands, pushing himself to stand upright on shaky pins. He shuffles down the hallway into the lounge. No-one is there.

'Hey Ben, you around?' he calls out in a croaky voice.

'You're up. In here, the kitchen.' Ben moves through the doorway to meet him. 'Wooo, shit, you don't look much better in daylight,' he laughs. 'Come into the kitchen, have some coffee. The girls are making brunch. You'll need some tucker, some sustenance to repair that body of yours.'

Toby accepts Kate's offer as she pulls a chair out from the table and he leans on her shoulder as he eases himself into a sitting position. 'Ta,' he says.

'Some toast and coffee to start? You poor thing,' Kate asks.

'Not that hungry,' Toby replies.

'Here, coffee, at least,' she says, pouring it for him

'We'd like you to stay until you're better,' Sharee says as she works at the stove. 'You have nowhere else to go, I guess.'

Toby nods. 'That's right,' he confirms in a mouse-like voice.

'Are there any friends you'd like us to contact? Let them know you're here? Your mum, perhaps?'

'No, no,' Toby hastily replies. 'No, not my mum. And I have no friends. It's been lonely writing at home. The guys from my neighbourhood prefer footy. Not writers, who they think are queer.'

Kate looks across at Sharee and purses her lips, as if she knows the type he's talking about.

'Yeah, we know what you mean,' Ben says. 'Plenty of them around here. Though there are some great surfie guys we like. They play footy and do other things as well. Some paint, and we know one that writes too. Terrific bloke.'

'So it's settled then,' Kate says chirpily. 'You'll stay here till you've recovered.'

Toby tries to smile, sipping at his coffee and nibbling on the toast Sharee has given him. She too sits down to eat.

'I'd offer you some of the Herald to read, but I don't think you could see it,' Ben laughs. Toby agrees.

'Not today, tomorrow maybe,' he says.

'You'll have to show us some of your book when you're better. Will that be okay?' Ben asks. Sharee kicks him under the table.

'Sure. You can look at it now. I don't mind. It's in my laptop. No password needed. Help yourself. Like to know what you think of it. It's been quite an effort.'

'Great, thanks. I like books, I want to write one myself, sometime,' Ben replies.

* * * * * * *

It takes Toby a week to get back to anything like himself, and in that time he learns that the paintings are Kate's. Sharee and Ben are at acting school. Their home is like a drop-in centre for all sorts of creative people. He can't quite believe such people exist, and that they share their love of the arts.

Each day, Kate walks with him along the beach, stopping to draw anything that catches her eye.

'You don't have to go,' she says. 'We all like you, we'd love you to stay.

Why don't you finish your book? I've been reading it. It's fabulous and anyway, you owe it to us. Otherwise we won't know how it ends. That's only fair.'

Toby is drawing an outline of Kate, in the sand with his big toe, then quickly erases it as she comes up behind him to look.

'Toby, you should let your Mum know you're safe. She will be worried.'

'No. I'll catch Betty on her way home after school. She can let my mum know I'm ok.'

* * * * * * *

He waits by one of the tortured plane trees, watching her as she skips through the gate with Sam in tow carrying her books, and Grace, her best girlfriend, also close by.

'Hey, Betty,' he calls, stepping out from behind the tree.

'Toby, Toby,' his sister yells, racing over to him. 'Wow, you're alright. I haven't stopped thinking about you. I'm so happy to see you.' Toby bends down and gives her a kiss on the cheek.

'How's things at home?' he asks.

'Pretty crappy,' she says. 'Mum and Phil aren't talking. She spends her days drinking. She'll be out of it when I get home.'

'Phil doesn't touch you, does he Betty?'

'Nah, he's too busy moping in front of the box. Has to get his own dinner. Mum's sure sad, Toby.'

'Tell her I'm okay, will you? Don't tell that fat pig, though.'

'Where are you living Toby? Can I come around to see you?'

'Not just yet. Give it some time. I've a whole bunch of friends who like me. I'm really happy. Gonna finish my book.'

'That's great. I want to read it too, Toby, don't forget me.'

'Sure, sis. Gotta go. Love you Betty. I'll come again next week to see how you are.'

She stands on tip-toes and flings her arms around him.

'Miss you Toby,' she says. 'I'll tell Mum you're good.'

'See you, Betty. Hey, Betty, you're Bella, in the book.'

'Wow, am I? I love Bella. Wow, that's so cool, Toby, so cool.'

'And Sam is Race.'

'Gee, don't know about that.'

'Come on, Betty, you like Sam.'

Betty laughs. 'I guess I do, but I don't know if I want to go on an

adventure with him.' They both laugh. 'See you, Toby.'
  'Yep, soon, eh?'

Chapter Thirteen

'Your ego's bloated. Give up. Call for help before it's too late. Or your fate will be linked to Zekai's.'

'Are you threatening me?' Zebu squealed, awkwardly rising from his chair, his fatty globules shaking.

Laxman, in the shadow of Zebu's likeness, held his ground. He rocked on his spindly legs, like a praying mantis. He leaned forward. Slime slapped against his ooze-dripping teeth. He sprang across the green puddle bubbling at his feet to meet Zebu.

'The Master-tree is ailing. It's suffering, the daughters are dying. We will all be dead if Acheron Afrit's roots perish. Trees from the outer-lands grow on the fringes of our city, multiplying in alarming numbers. The carbon dioxide is being replaced. Can't you smell it? Oxygen is seeping into Lair City.'

The Mancirian's head emitted weird sounds. His tongue flicked wildly like a whip around Laxman's weaving body. The Jaar's flexibility stunned Zebu, an attribute the Mancirian hadn't realised before. The Jaar moved in a circle around Zebu, fortunate to survive Dr Steel's flaying metal fingers, which sent sparks into the grey carbon air.

'It's your likeness. You're too busy preening yourself in its abominable shadow to see we are under attack by a silent enemy. Jaars no longer accept your self-proclaimed rule. There is no alliance,' Laxman shouted, easily springing well out of range of Zebu's gruesome tongue, as Dr Steel minced its way spinning, tripping, unable to get close to the Jaar.

'Half of your Lairs are dead. Terminated by storms. Storms caused by your fires in the outer lands. Those you have left must be let loose on the trees that are marching towards Lair City. Act now, and the Jaars will leave you alone, otherwise your likeness will be destroyed.'

Trembling, Zebu stamped his claws into the concrete floor, cracking small shards away under his furious weight. 'The Lairs are mine and will do my bidding, and that will be to feed all Jaars to the Master-tree's greedy gut,' Zebu screamed, spitting balls of toxic phlegm. They whistled past Laxman, who was manoeuvring himself down the Library steps. Both Zebu and Dr Steel, in aggressive pursuit, abruptly halted at the sight of fifty Jaars, mouths prised apart, collectively screaming, ascending the steps with ropes swinging from their spindly fingers, racing towards Zebu's likeness, ready to fasten the cords tight around the wooden edifice. Some bounced towards Zebu and Steel, and with snarling, screeching howls drove both backwards against the Library wall. The Mancirian lashed out, swinging his talon claws, while Steel's fingers slashed, expanding, working in a frenzy without success. The Jaars were constantly on the move, darting forward, landing kicks on their corralled victims while those who had Oak tethered heaved on the ropes.

Laxman bellowed at them to pull the idol down, screaming for its destruction. Neke, trapped by their fury, hid, coiling her herself up under the carved overhanging globules, afraid of being discovered while the Jaars grunted at their labour.

'Pull harder,' Laxman urged, but Oak could not be budged. She stood anchored, secure in her roots.

Laxman's face was tortured as he yelled angrily for more effort, but it was becoming obvious the task was too difficult, beyond his charges. He dropped his end of the rope and glared at Zebu, who was still fending off the attack. He called the Jaars to his side, a mistake fatal for two whose concentration had lapsed for a split second. Zebu's wrath exploded and his talon hand caught the side of one's neck, startling another who turned into the snapping fingers of Dr Steel.

Parting an escape route amongst the fleeing Jaars, Zebu inched forward, picking up one of the dead and lifting the body above his head. To the horror of the seething mass who watched, he sent the body bouncing across the floor, skidding to a halt at their feet. A nervous chatter broke out among their ranks, then a jittery high-pitched squeal of, 'Lairs, Lairs.'

Laxman turned to see them, too many to count, blocking any hope of escape. The Jaars moved like a swarming nest of flying ants, bashing into each other as the Lairs squeezed them closer into a corner. Dr Steel, in its element, relishing its work, chopped away, destroying the

Jaars until they were nothing but a mangled heap, till only Laxman stood.

'Leave him to me,' Zebu hollered.

Laxman watched the Mancirian untie the rope from his likeness.

'You won't need that,' the Jaar demurred quietly. 'I will throw myself to Acheron Afrit.'

'Then come here,' Zebu yelled. And Laxman walked to him, stepping over the bodies of his own kind. The Mancirian slapped the Jaar to the ground, planted his claw foot upon him and roared in delight.

'Drag the Jaars to their tree. Let's celebrate the greatness of Manci,' Zebu called gleefully.

The Lairs gathered the fallen, flung them over their shoulders and minced down the staircase, thrilled at the prospect of the entertainment they were soon to have. They had never liked the Jaars. That their aloof superiority was silenced now for good brought about a joviality, a good humour, unknown before in Lair City.

They piled the corpses high near the swaying tree and waited as Zebu dragged Laxman like a trophy through the buzzing carnival atmosphere, patting his Lairs, praising them, as he waddled past. He dropped Laxman roughly and pinned him under his claw, once more screwing his face into the ground.

'There's your Master-tree. Do you think it will hear your stupid prayers?' he asked.

'Acheron Afrit is all-knowing. It will always hear our words.'

Zebu laughed.

'Lairs wish you comfort,' one said, while two others placed Zebu's chair, retrieved from the Library Portico. The Mancirian's mood took another leap as he reclined, ready for the offerings of torn Jaars.

Laxman lifted his head. 'Can't you smell the oxygen pushing its way into Lair City?' he pleaded.

Zebu slammed the Jaar's body back down.

'You're disgusting. Accept your fate. Dr Steel, let's show this maggot how much meat his tree desires.'

Steel's fingers clicked together. Its screen rolled as it moved towards the Jaar remains. A cheer filled the narrow street as it hurled the first body at the tree's base. The tree opened its crater-like mouth and the Jaar disappeared into the crevice.

'Hahaha, look at this. It's wonderful,' Zebu beamed as Laxman struggled to turn his head away. The Lairs were beside themselves, dancing on their awkward limbs.

Five, six, seven – in they went. The tree gurgled, belched, chomped. Its boughs vibrated, its thorns curled, almost lancing the Orabanche sliding around in its top branches. The Orabanche was raving, thrilled beyond description. 'See, see, you farting bag of gas,' he said. 'Jaars, haha, yes, yes, and look, a Mancirian laying them to waste. If only I had my snake to give to him now, I'd be free of your rotten, stinking branches.'

Lair voices rattled against the buildings, spurring Dr Steel on. The Orabanche, hanging by its tail, slobbering, was unaware that the Lairs had spotted it and were pointing, screaming, believing it had crawled out of the tree from the bowels of the Undercity.

Without warning, the tree let out a terrible belch; putrid gases billowed from its mouth. Its whole structure shuddered as it started regurgitating the Jaar bodies, hurtling them back into the carbon. Bodies rained down on the mesmerised gathering, tipping the foul, deformed lizard from its perch, sending it spiralling, wheeling into the Master-tree's fathomless pit.

Zebu struggled from his chair, shocked, ducking out of the way of the undigested Jaars tossed by the tree, splattering all around him. Released from Zebu's weight, Laxman rolled over, sprang to his feet, and fled, green tears falling from his cat-slit eyes. He disappeared into the oily, shadowed streets, bent, crippled by the sight of the dreadful events he'd witnessed. Pain rippled across his skull. Visions of revenge rang through his bones. Zebu's voice trailed a booming cry after him.

* * * * * * *

Oak's roots flexed, sending cracks throughout Silk's apartment walls. Chunks of concrete, then clumps of dirt, fell as the tree wriggled, shifting her base. Silk felt trepidation sneak into her heart.

'The Truth Stream moves against Lair City,' she whispered. Gaps started to appear, long fissures tracing Oak's roots back up to the Library steps. Silk climbed through the roots and peered into the open vents. She could feel a rush of oxygen being sucked from her room and past her head, racing towards the city.

'Oak, I will tell the people to prepare,' she called, as she manoeuvred herself around the lacework of Oak's roots. Heading back to the floor, she was staggered to find Neke blocking her way. She rubbed at her eyes.

'Is it truly you?' she asked, 'tell me that you're not a vision. I see you so often in my dreams.'

'Oxygen is being restored above ground. The Alien is out of his depth. I've come for your pure heart, to return it to where it belongs. This is no mirage,' Neke cooed, climbing around Silk's outstretched arms.

'Epic, Solo and the Kuaha are marching amongst Oak's offspring as we speak. Others, children of nature led by Keywee and Powerflower marshal the Truth Stream. Your people must have courage. They will triumph. The battle begins.'

* * * * * * *

Zebu thrashed his bulbous head around, sniffing at the carbon. At last, he caught scent of it. Oxygen!

He stomped towards Acheron Afrit, snatching several Lairs by their coats. He cast them at the tree's base, bellowing for it to stuff itself. The tree stood swaying, its smooth bark radiating a crimson heat, smouldering from its boughs, rejecting the offerings. The Lairs simply gained their feet and minced away as quickly as they could, inching around the carnage of broken bodies that lay silent, spread out across Data Street. Zebu started to panic. He screamed to Dr Steel to get him humans. Now! Then he spun around violently and bellowed 'I'll come with you. Get my vest,'

'What about Laxman?' Steel asked.

'The Jaar is alone. We will pull it apart and eat it ourselves, like all of these,' he spat, pouncing on one and dissected it with his clawed feet. 'First, we have to feed that!' he screamed, pointing at Acheron Afrit, 'or my city will choke.'

* * * * * * *

Oak felt Epic's presence before she heard his words. Her expanding limbs exploded, knocking away any likeness of Zebu. Her trunk shot skyward, doubling in height, sending forth a cloud of new green leaves, creating an aura of sparkling light and fresh air, pushing aside the sticky grey carbon dioxide. So rapid was Oak's conversion, her incarnation, Epic had to be careful not to lose his sense of balance in the mysteries of life.

'Oak, you astound me. Remind me again of your knowledge.'

'Epic, without the Superbird Race, we are incomplete. But with you we are whole. The land cries out for our success. I hear it now, advancing on this vile city. And the chants of the Kuaha, the Gatekeepers, brings sap back into my heart. My wounds I can outgrow. My memory is strong. The Truth Stream cannot be subjugated to any creature's will. For we are symbiotic, reliant on each other. The Mancirian goes below to collect humans for its own end. It thinks it farms this world. It has no understanding of fellowship. No care for any other than itself. It is doomed by its own Alien needs.'

'Your words are perfectly true, like your being, Oak. Soon the Superbird Race will dwell again in sight of all, in the shelter of your towering life force, safe, free. No longer exiles, imprisoned in rock.'

'Epic, you'd best go, for Zebu is on the move with his henchman Dr Steel. He has smelt the change in the air and thinks the Jaar's tree needs more sacrifices, more human blood. Laxman knows the tree will hibernate now, reject all offerings. No longer will it generate carbon dioxide. The city is filling with oxygen. Can you taste it, feel it in your wings?

'The Mancirian is tyrannical, too obsessed to see the warning signs, and Laxman prowls the city, searching for his only chance of survival – the key to the cosmic communicator which Zebu has hidden. The Jaar must not find it nor the Mancirian use it. I have watched Zebu turn it in his talons, gloat at its wonder, then disappear into the Library. It must be close by. Epic, you must find it. Lay claim to it first.'

Chapter Fourteen

Life is so different now for Toby. He grows inside the encouragement of his friends, especially Kate. He has the house to himself most days, and can be found on the sunporch, trying to finish some part of his book before sunset. He prints off each chapter as he goes, leaving it on the kitchen table for the others to read.

Ben and Sharee are about to do their first play together and opening night is upon them. Kate and Toby sit in the front row, cheering, pleased for their friends.

Kate has brought flowers. Leaping from her seat at the end of the play, she throws her flowers onto the stage, applauding wildly. There is to be an after-party at the house. Lots of folk are coming, the director, the producer and the rest of the cast and their friends, and of course Ben and Sharee's.

'Weren't they fab?' Kate is saying as she and Toby walk from the theatre towards their house. 'I knew Ben would steal the show,' she says. Toby just listens, his hands shoved into his pockets, looking at Kate.

'Do you want to see my studio? It's in this block. I don't normally let people see what I'm doing, but it would be interesting to know what you think,' she says in a serious voice, turning to look at him. 'It'll be a while before the party begins. They have to get out of their costumes, remove their make-up, be interviewed, all those things. Come on, I'll show you.'

The studio is on the ground floor at the back of a four-storey building. She grabs his hand and leads him down a service lane. The touch of her warm hand sends a thrilling charge throughout his body. He is scared. He wants her, wants to tell her that he thinks he loves her, but he is frightened. What if she rejects his advances? What if she says

'Oh, Toby, I only want to be your friend'?

No, he thinks, best keep it to myself. He withdraws his hand, immediately regretting it. She pulls the keys from her jeans and opens the door. The studio is so much larger than he thought it would be – in fact, it's huge. The smell of paint, linseed oil and turps fills his nose. Giant canvases line the walls, brushes stand in jars all over the place, the floor is splattered with bright colourful patterns made from random spills.

'What do you reckon?' she asks quickly, searching his eyes for a response.

He is perplexed by her output, her energy, overwhelmed by the sheer size of the works. Massive detailed landscapes alive with creatures, humans tending gardens, leading horses, women hanging washing, children splashing in streams. The vitality of her brushwork, the rhythm connecting each corner to the central figures at work or play in different poses; the paint thick, luminous, alive.

'Kate, they're amazing. I feel I could walk inside them. They reminds me of the Truth Stream. How the Truth Stream would be.'

Kate smiles. 'I'm so glad you like them,' she says walking over to move one, exposing another canvas of equal size.

Toby's eyes nearly leave their sockets. 'It's Superbird,' he whispers. 'Superbird in the Truth Stream with Keywee, Powerflower, Bella, Race and Solo.'

'Yes,' Kate says. 'I hope you like it.'

'Like it? Like it? I'm stunned, Kate. Truly blown away. It's just as I imagined. I mean, the way I'd have painted it if I could. How? When?'

'After I started reading your book. It excited me. I found it inspirational. See, I've used you as the model for Solo, though I've made your hair longer.'

'Kate, what can I say? You too... you... well... you move me, too.'

Kate looks at her hands, then around the room. 'That's... that's...'

'That's what?' Toby asks, stepping closer to her.

'That's what I want,' she replies shyly, and reaches out and hugs him, wrapping her arms tightly around him.

Her body pressed against his feels so good.

'I think about you all the time,' she says. 'It's distracting. Some days I just sit here doing little doodles of you. Can't get you off my mind.'

'I feel the same, Kate. It's been impossible to write.'

'Come on,' she says, slipping her hand into his. 'Let's go home. The party will be in full swing by now.' This time he doesn't let go.

* * * * * * *

The house is buzzing, crammed with people. Music greets them as they stroll in through the door.

'Kate, Kate,' Sharee calls out from across the room. 'You're here, hey, Toby, come on, get a drink.'

'You guys were terrific. Magic. The play was brilliant,' Kate squeals, embracing Sharee. 'Where's Ben?'

'He's in the kitchen,' Sharee laughs, 'holding court, lapping up his fame. There's a few toffs from broadcasting fattening his ego, asking him to audition for a new series they have planned. He's in seventh heaven. Don't think he'll come down for weeks. Hey, hold on, what's going on? You two look decidedly happy.'

Kate jumps up and kisses Toby on the lips.

'Yep, we are. Very,' she says.

Toby smiles at Sharee. 'Yep, totally.'

'Your dealer's here Kate, walking through the house complaining he's never seen this or that work before. How come? he wanted to know. Thinks you've been hiding work from him. He's trying to sell it to Holden Ford. He's dragging him around, singing your praises. Telling him to buy while he can, that soon your prices will double. It's quite a laugh. Have fun, babe. I'm going back into the kitchen to catch up with my thespian. I think he thinks he's the new Anthony Hopkins being offered a newly discovered play by Harold Pinter, already about to accept his academy award.'

'Kate,' her dealer calls, pushing his way towards her, holding his drink high above his head. 'Kate, you naughty child. You've been keeping things from me.'

'Warwick, this is Toby, my boyfriend.'

Warwick nods. 'Now, Kate, you only have a few weeks until your show. Tell me that you're up to it.'

Kate winks at her dealer, and grabs Toby's hand. 'See you later,' she says. 'Have a great night. Mix, Warwick. There are quite a few other artists here,' she says, walking away. 'God, he can be a pain. Let's skip through to the kitchen. I want to see Ben.' She pulls Toby along, stopping to say hi to others along the way. 'Wow,' she whispers in Toby's ear. 'Look at these heavy hitters, big players from Earth

Publications and other publishing houses. They're friends of Mark's, the director of Ben's play. You should meet some of them.' Toby backs away. 'Come on, they won't bite.'

'No, no, Kate. Please. It's just not me.'

'Don't be silly… Hi, Gerald, meet Toby. He's a novelist, has a great work you should read. Not far from being finished.'

'Pleased to meet you, Toby, what's your book about?'

'Lairs and Mancirians, creatures from other worlds,' Toby meekly answers. 'The end of old ways, and new beginnings, I guess.'

'Ahhh, traditional myths. Quite the thing today. Drop your manuscript around. Here's my card. Now, Kate, how's your painting? Still making works too big for people's homes?'

'Bigger, Gerald. Though I'm sure you could fit one in your mansion. Make sure you come to my next show.'

'Sure will, honey. You're looking good. Must be Toby here that's put such a blush on your dial. Nice to meet you Toby. Don't forget to drop your book off. We're always looking for new talent.'

'See, that wasn't so bad. Gerald's a nice guy. Come on, let's give Ben a bit of tagging. He looks like he's going to fly away. Got to keep him grounded, else we won't be able to eat toast with him in the morning. Won't get him off the ceiling.'

'I'm already floating on the roof, Kate. Just being next to you is so special. I've never known this feeling before.'

She kisses him again, touches his cheek. 'Thanks, Toby, I feel the same way.'

They spend the night together. Ben has collapsed earlier, good-heartedly blind drunk. Sharee has tucked him up in bed, planting a kiss on his forehead, saying 'good night, Mr Brando, sleep tight,' and gone back to keep company with the few stragglers who plan to keep partying till the dawn.

'You will take your book to Gerald, won't you?' Kate asks when their lust has been sated. Toby, rolling around the bed in delight, says, 'That was fantastic, elevating beyond this world. I want some more.'

Kate flings herself on top of him. 'No, listen. I'm serious. You will, won't you? Show him your story.'

'I don't know, Kate. I don't know if it's any good. It's just something I had to write, to get out of me. I never thought beyond that.'

'Well, Toby Miller, it's better than good.'

'You have to say that.'

'Ha ha,' she laughs. 'No, really. Ben and Sharee also talk about it. We all want to know how it finishes. Tell me what made you write such a chilling story of a world lost in such darkness, and horrible creatures from the stars. Where did it come from? It's so creepy at times, yet wonderful, imaginative, a total universe.'

'I guess it started with Phil, Mum's new man after Dad left. He reminded me of a programmed horror, not quite human. Cruel. It's hard to define. And Betty, my little sister. I knew she felt trapped, unhappy. She wanted Dad back so much it was difficult to watch. And Phil's mates came, taking over the house. Sub-human jerks, drunken, outlandish creeps who slurred their words. And Mum sinking, lost, turning into one of them. No longer the Mum who brought me up. Under Phil's ugly thumb.

'That's where I got the idea for the Lairs' fingers stretching, mangling Betty's and my world. And Uncle Bob, not really an uncle, who came around to get into Mum's pants when Phil wasn't around. Bob, through his cunning and wealth, controlled Phil in the most despicable way, without Phil even knowing.

'So Bob became the Mancirian Zekai Manci in my mind. He's a big boy in the money world, got his fingers in every pie, developments, reclaimed land, you know the kind. Doesn't give a shit about the environment or anyone else, only his own interests. A real maniac. That's where it started, and as I went along, it grew into its own skin. I watched TV a lot, mainly the news, docos and realised it wasn't just Bob. There's a whole league of similar tyrants, arseholes helping him destroy our world.

'I watched a programme on indigenous people. They fascinated me, the way they lived close to the land, hunting for wood pigeons and other creatures, hunting some close to extinction. I thought, imagine if it wasn't so. If one of the birds became a Superbird and spoke to them, told them to stop such terrible things and they heard, became their protectors, and kept records of that day.

'They tattooed their faces, these indigenous people. Ink markings that told of their heritage, their place in the world. And I thought, let's make it the Superbirds that make these markings on their faces with their wings. Begin the tradition, give them back their souls and, of course, then they could see how the forests and animals were integral to their lives and set about making it right.

'And all the stuff on the news spoke of floods, ghastly deeds, fires, innocent life destroyed by wars, hunger, deprivation. The list is endless. Nuclear bombs, the race for energy, greenhouse gases, environmental footprints. I don't know where to stop. I could go on, but you know what I'm saying.

'Humanity has lost control. No thought for the future. We've lost our love of nature. Money, that's all that's important. It's how we measure our power. And greed knows no bounds. If the last dollar was to be made out of the last tree standing, we would cut it down. Still, there are those that fight to save the world. I wanted to save Betty and her friends. That's why I wanted to write the book.

'So I invented Solo as my hero, Nua, Otahi and his clan, and I wanted, dreamed of, a better place that we could grow into from the Undercity, that dark place I felt we lived in. I guess my life felt like I lived in Lair City, working for the Mancirians, people like Bob. I wanted to rebel, so I refused to get a job and decided to write about it. But it took on a life of its own. Now I don't know any more. Since meeting you, Ben and Sharee, your friends, I feel different, uplifted. I've escaped into a place that has shown me more, that people do care, that love is real.'

'Toby darling, you are free. You're with us. I love you, love you so much I could eat you.'

'God, Kate, don't say that. Humans are Zekai's favourite food. I don't want to wake up falling down the Chute into one of his holding tanks, ready to be devoured.'

'You're a strange boy,' Kate laughs, 'then I'll just lick you instead,' she says, diving under the covers.

Later, Kate says, 'Your life's been rather rotten since your dad left. Do you ever wish you could see him?'

'Sure I do, but I don't know where he's gone.'

'Gee, I thought he might have tried to come and see you and Betty. How come? Why not?'

'I think that was the worst, maybe even more shitty than Phil. I guess that ratified my belief that the world was such an ugly place.'

'He might have tried,' Kate suggests, 'but could have been turned away. These things do happen. You should try and find him.'

'I wouldn't know where to start, Kate.'

Chapter Fifteen

'I can't believe I'm back in this hated place.' Nua's tattooed face is red with anger. His head feathers shake outside his top knot. He is tearing strips, berating the hapless warriors, who move closer to Chief Otahi while I try to calm him as best I can.

'It's too late now, Nua,' I urge, 'we can't change what has happened. Your men are as mortified as you are. All your insight and warnings have escaped into the city with him. We agree this death could have been avoided. Yes, we should have listened to you before we set out. We should have ended the traitor's life. It is hard for us to contemplate Jall's work. Manu was loved by us all, but it would be foolish of us to go blindly pursuing Jall.'

'How did it happen? You were never to take your eyes off him,' Nua shrieks. 'Now he will be with the Aliens, passing on our numbers, and plans. Our surprise attack is worthless. Lairs will now be lying in wait at each turn.'

Chief Otahi places his hand on Nua. 'Brother, do not take out your rage on your own people. Save it for those who deserve it. Accept that Jall has escaped.'

'No! I will track him. He must be stopped before he reaches the Mancirian.'

'Then I shall listen to you. I won't make the same mistake twice. If you must go, then go with my blessings. We will follow the line of Oak's life-giving trees. But be warned. Our scouts still find pockets of foul air, the city is still thick with carbon dioxide, and they have seen many Lairs cutting into Oak's children. We will have to confront them. It will slow us down.'

'I will come with you,' I say to Nua.

'That would please me, Solo. Your memory of the city will be a great advantage.'

We leave Chief Otahi and his band of sixty warriors with apprehension in their eyes, conversing under one of Oak's trees. Those who have been in Lair City before, those that have fought the Lairs, calmly talk to the others, strategising their attack, discussing the Lairs' abilities, telling how best to avoid their extending fingers and hideous kicks.

'They are slow and clumsy,' Otahi says, 'but their strength and size can be a shock and their numbers can make your heart skip a beat. Still, you are Kuaha. Let's not forget that. Work together, separate them and knock them down by taking out their kneecaps. Get them to the ground then you will have a clear shot at their screens. We will leave in groups. Within each group there will be one of us who has fought them before. You fight the battle of all battles. Remember you fight for the Truth Stream.'

As the two of us move away from the Kuaha and into the city, I feel a sense of foreboding hanging over the foreign landscape of concrete buildings and Rim-railed streets. The collecting carbon drips from above, spiralling down on to the side-walks in tar-bogs, evil gunk that has to be avoided. Nua and I dart from one tree to the next, clinging to doorways, down back alleyways, testing the air. Repelled at times, we have to retreat, retrace our progress through the maze of Lair City.

How chilling it is to hear the sound of metal on wood echoing through the gloom and, before long, we come upon its source. Small groups are feverishly hacking into Oak's children, a laborious task that has the Lairs fuming and cursing. The stubborn trunks and boughs deflect every chop.

'No, not that way,' I whisper into Nua's ear as he moves towards the Lairs. I lead him through the entrance of the nearest building. Its windows smashed by falling limbs, which allows oxygen to penetrate its hallways and the tiniest glimmer of light to help us to see our way.

We sneak past, inch our way forward between each fractured window. The Lairs are furiously working at the branches. A sound like wild pigs grunting escapes their voice-boxes.

We are leaning against a column when Nua taps my shoulder and jerks his head in the direction of the floor. A few feet in front of us lies a dark, tangled heap blocking our path. At first, I think it is part of a tree, a branch that has come straight through a window to rest here inside the building, an amputation spilling resin around its lifeless form. Then I see Nua bend down to pick up parts of Jall's Kuaha clothing. Flax skirt and sandals, his dogskin cape concealing the grotesque naked body of a Lair, pooled in its own thick, oily blood. How strange it is to think it was once human like us. Its sausage-like toes and fingers shrivelled, its boxed-head, far too big for its body, is cracked, oozing liquid from its seams.

'Jall is now dressed as a Lair,' Nua hisses. 'He has the Lair's converter and will be able to move in the carbon dioxide, move about among the Lairs. He could be outside this building lying in wait for us. I don't like it. My eyes are stinging. Every nerve tells me there is no oxygen at the end of this hall. Is there another route?'

'We must make for the Library; that's where he will go. He will be searching for the Alien, wanting rewards for himself,' I say, grabbing at Nua and leading him back to where we entered, frustrated with our progress but relieved to be standing once again under cover of one of Oak's offspring.

The air grows colder, mist curls, steams from our mouths, and nostrils. Thunder and lightening split the sky, then the leaves overhead are pummelled, battered by hail. They recoil as balls of ice ricochet, bouncing off and through the branches of the tree we are sheltering beneath.

I have to shout to be heard above the din.

'I'm freezing,' I yell to Nua. 'I'll freeze to the spot if we don't get a move on. The Truth Stream sure is angry.'

'And dangerous,' Nua bellows back. 'These hailstones are large enough to knock one stupid or crack one's skull.'

'At least the Lairs won't be out in it. They will be driven into the buildings' doorways, saving Oak's offspring from their cruel onslaught,' I scream. 'Let's take our chances.'

'Okay.'

We sprint for the nearest building, fending off the stinging balls, our arms above our heads, our numb fingers taking a beating. Slipping, skidding on the marble-carpeted street, I yelp, lose my balance, tripping to slide boots-first against the sidewalk. Nua scoops me up by my collar, slings me in one flowing action back onto my feet, propelling us both into the building's entrance and respite from the pounding hail that shatters into smaller pieces of itself. I flap my arms, wring my hands to regain feeling in them. Nua also complains, busily rubbing his together and doing a little jig. His sandalled feet are blue with cold.

'Let's move from tree to tree down this avenue,' Nua suggests, after poking his head around the side of the building. None of Oak's children have been attacked here, so it's possible no Lairs are nearby. Come on, Solo.' He dives out of the doorway to the first tree. It does at least afford some protection. I cling close to its trunk, wanting the storm to cease, though aware it is working in our favour however brutal that favour may be.

I squeeze myself around the tree, trying to find a better path, perhaps an alcove further down, only to see a pack of Lairs huddled inside the building opposite. Their screens glaring back at us from one of the gutted windows. I jump with fright, alerting Nua to their presence. We scramble towards the next tree, some fifty feet away. Thankfully the hail is now easing to sleet and by the time we make the following tree, snow begins to fall. Soft flakes that shimmer, drifting through the calamitous flashes of the electrical storm, dressing the city in a crisp white gown.

Lairs, scores of them, now appear from every nook and doorway. Their screens seem queer – dull, curious mumblings seep from their voice boxes as they shuffle out into the snow. We watch them come to a standstill, one by one, wobble and fall to their knees then onto their screens, with muffled little pleas. Enveloped by the snow.

'What's happening to them?' Nua asks.

'I'm not sure.' Then it clicks. 'Lairs are cold-blooded creatures. The fluids in the bodies have frozen. It's too cold for them to function,' I say gleefully.

'What will happen as the snow thaws?' he asks. 'Will they reactivate, come alive?'

'No, no, no.' I laugh. 'They are finished. As the snow melts, the water will contaminate their circuits. They will fuse and die. That's how Zapper and Rink finished off Dr Thrasha. They lured him out into an electrical storm to be soaked in rain. How I wish we could have saved Rink and Zapper. They both deserved much better fates. It was their movement – the beginning of the Lairlights, Rink's curiosity about Oak – that started the demise of Lair City, giving us the chance to change its shape.'

'And Lek,' Nua added, 'that poor creature rotting in snail slime. So many have paid the ultimate price. We also free the Undercity for him. And Ubu. Listen, Solo, I hear his voice on the wind. No, truly, listen. Your dog's spirit accompanies us.'

It hurts my heart to hear his name. Of all that I have lost, his faithful friendship I miss the most. His absolute trust and protective aggression saved both of us in battle. I so wanted to hear his bark. I found myself straining my ears as Nua was doing.

'Do you hear him?' Nua asks. 'He's watching over us. I know it.'

'Yes, yes I can, Nua. He is with us on this march. Look, there's his shadow. See his tail bristling against that wall up ahead, leading us safely on.'

I look back towards the snail cages where I know Otahi will be hunkered down, waiting for the storm to subside. I cry out in astonishment as, there in the east, a blue band of sky peeps through the falling snow.

'Nua,' I yell. 'Look, the Truth Stream sky has crossed the Great River. It's pushing the curtain of alien carbon aside. This is more than we could ever have hoped for. And Ubu by our side. The city is filling with sweet air. Can you taste its freshness? Can you?' I turn to ask him, but Nua is striding forward. I have to run to catch up. He is turning Lairs over, checking their boxed screens.

'What are you doing?'

'I'm looking for Jall,' he spits.

'Jall is not cold-blooded,' I say.

'Oh, how wrong you are Solo,' he replies.

'Nua, he won't be among these Lairs. He will be moving, like us, towards the Library. This weather won't slow him down. We should still be careful. Who knows what other creatures the Alien has hidden away.'

'Then let's go and find out. My club is itching to do some damage.'

The streets are dotted with Lairs, covered or being covered by the continuous flakes. Like zombies, still emerging from whatever cover they had sought, to flop into the increasing drifts. It is unbelievable, eerie. The black tar that has collected above us on the towering monoliths and ledges of the city is now under sheets of glowing white crystals. I keep peering back over my shoulder, excited by the widening slice of cobalt sky.

'I've found him,' Nua's voice sings. 'See, here are his footprints.' A line of impressions can be seen leading away, towards the Library. 'He's running. Look how far apart each step is.' The marks are slowly being obliterated by the snow. 'We almost have him, Solo,' Nua enthuses.

I caution Nua. 'There is no guarantee. There still might be pockets of carbon dioxide,' I plead. 'Two gulps of its poison will burn your lungs out, finish you off like the Lairs scattered around us.' Though agitated, he slows to a pace I feel more comfortable with.

* * * * * * *

I see a movement out of the corner of my eye, and stop abruptly. Nua senses it too. He spins, lifting his club above his head, tongue poking forward from his lips. Small scurrying noises are moving behind us, hidden amongst the lifeless bodies of the Lairs. I shiver, expecting to see Jall spring out towards us. Nua has no fear. He smiles at last, and run towards the first corpse, ready to meet his hated foe front on, only to send a fox fleeing from its cover and a rabbit springing into the air.

It is apparent that the snow around us is teeming with wildlife from the Truth Stream, creatures following us, pouring into the city to witness its destruction, keeping a safe distance, tracking in our wake. We both begin to laugh.

'We are not alone in our quest,' Nua says, dropping his club to his side. 'Our army increases tenfold.'

We take a step. They too, take a step. We stop. They too, do the same, obviously a little frightened yet needing to see for themselves the end of the Alien rule. Or perhaps they know we will not lead them into harm's way and are here to bolster our spirits, letting us know they approve, willing us forward, reminding us that this is also for them. After all, we are the Gatekeepers. More and more creatures of different varieties and breeds, large and small, are arriving.

We follow Jall's footsteps to where I know they will lead. Past Oak's children, sprouting, lifting back the tarmac, unfurling under the Truth Stream's sky, gathering pigeons and owls in their branches. Fantails flitter excitedly, singing joyous calls above our heads, songs from the forest, rivers and hills.

'There he is,' I say to Nua as we stand on the far side of the quadrangle looking at the Library and Jall's telltale steps. And there is Oak herself in full flight, waving her clustered branches in a thrilling display, bursting with a profusion of flowers, telling us the air is safe.

Chapter Sixteen

Toby finishes his book. He prints out and leaves the last chapter on the bedside table for Kate to read. She photocopies the lot, binds it in her studio, places a note inside it. *The Birth of Superbird*, by Toby Miller, it says, and she takes it around to Gerald's office. He is busy, so she leaves it with his secretary, saying, 'Please make sure Gerald gets it. It's a novel he has asked to see.'

Then, back to her studio to finish the last painting for her upcoming show. Her dealer is waiting outside. He is a little put out as she is late, having forgotten their appointment at midday. It is now closer to one, and his mood is somewhat short.

'I'm sorry, Warwick,' she pleads. 'Had to run an errand.'

'Jesus, Kate, there's more to the world than Kate Carlton.'

'Yes, okay, Warwick, I'm sorry. What more can I say?' She opens up the studio. He steps in.

'Why do you have to paint so large?' he moans. 'How am I going to move them? Paint smaller, Kate, for godsake.'

He circles the work, umming and ahhing, tilting his head to the side, fingers to his lips, lights a cigarette, tips his head back to blow out the smoke.

'Not bad, not bad at all. Fresh, interesting. Think I'll be able to sell one to Holden Ford. That's a start. You will need to have them down at the Gallery early. Be a lot of work to hang them.'

'I want to be involved. It's important to me, the order. There's a sequence I need to see them in.'

'Yes, yes, don't worry. You can. You're such a precious lot, you artists, but I understand. Just don't be late, okay?'

He is about to leave when he sees the edge of another painting, just peeping out from behind what he has been viewing. 'What's that?' he asks, moving towards it. 'You still hiding things from me?'

'It's something personal. Not finished. Not ready to be seen.'

'Come on Kate, it's me, your dealer. Your friend. You can show me.'

She hesitates, thinking it is so different from her present work and she isn't sure if she should show it to him.

'Come on, come on,' he chirps, and starts moving the covering work himself. 'Looks different for you. The colours are quite dark.' She races over.

'Let me do it. Step back,' she says, kind of snappy.

'My god Kate! Where did you drag this up from? It's…It's…well, baffling, but intriguing. What's it about? Really like the atmosphere. Feels historical, like Cook's landing, except the creatures. They're fantastic, like none I've ever seen. Come on, out with it, what is it about?'

'It's a work inspired by Toby. You remember Toby, I introduced him to you the other night at the party?.'

'Oh, your boyfriend.'

'Yes, him. He's a novelist, and it's inspired by his latest novel *The Birth of Superbird*. He's hoping to get it published. They're looking at it now.'

'Who are?'

'Earth Publications.'

'Really?'

'Yes.'

'Hey, that could be fabulous. We could launch a show of your work and have the book launch at the same time.'

'Hold up, Warwick, let's do one show at a time.'

'Yes, I guess you're right. I'm jumping ahead of myself, but it's a great idea. Think about it. Ask Toby.'

* * * * * * *

Kate's big night arrives. Toby says he'll meet her at the gallery, that he'll come down with Ben and Sharee. Ben lends him a tie. Sharee loops it for him, pulling it to his collar. 'Man, you look smart,' she coos.

Toby is shocked. He didn't expect to see such a massive crowd. People pulling up in Mercs, even Bentleys, dressed to the nines, met by a snappily attired doorman who bows, greeting them at the door. Inside, people are drinking tall flutes of champagne.

Kate, dressed to kill, looks stunning. She makes her way through the crowd and kisses Toby.

'All but two sold,' she whispers excitedly. 'Warwick's wetting his pants, calling everyone darling. It's such a scream. I have to go and mingle. You do understand?'

'Of course,' Toby says, holding the glass she hands to him as she slips away.

Ben and Sharee are mobbed at once, so Toby walks around the walls to check the titles, then sees the prices and nearly faints. $30,000 for this one, another $23,000, and little red dots beside all but two.

Warwick, now carrying another red dot on the end of his finger, moves Toby out of the way, and, smiling from ear to ear, is about to rejoin his clients when he recognises Toby.

'You're Toby, Kate's bloke,' he says. 'Kate's such a talent. I love her.'

'Yep,' Toby replies as the dealer glides off.

Then a voice says 'Toby Miller, what are you doing here? Not your sort of place, I'd have thought.'

He turns to see his family doctor grinning back at him. 'Oh, Dr Marsh. How are you?'

'Well, Toby, a box of birds. Hope for you the same?'

'Yep, I'm well, thanks.'

'Ahh, your dad will be happy to know that, Toby.'

'Have you seen him, Doctor?'

'Well, yes Toby. I treated him. He's much improved. I thought you would have known that.'

'What do you mean you've treated him, he's on the mend? What was wrong with him?'

'Oh, Toby. Your father tried to kill himself, Toby. Didn't your mother tell you?'

'I haven't seen Dad for three years. Since he left Mum, walked out on us.'

'I'm so sorry. He…he found it very difficult not seeing you kids. Please forgive me. I can see from your face your mother didn't tell you. I'm sorry, Toby. This is most unprofessional of me. I shouldn't have been the one to tell you.'

'It's okay, Dr Marsh. You weren't to know.'

'Look, Toby, he's as fit as a fiddle again. Has a new life. He's seeing someone. I think it's the real thing, if you get my drift. He's happy, well adjusted, doesn't need me any more. You should go see him. He's just in the next village up the coast. Come around to the clinic. I'll give you his address.'

'Thanks, Dr Marsh. I will.'

'Anyhow, son, have you grown an interest in the arts?'

'Kate, Kate Carlton. She's my girlfriend. I live with her.'

'Goodness me, Toby, that's just great. Fantastic. Good on you. I've bought a work. It's for the clinic. Maybe you could introduce us. I've never met her, just watched her work consolidate, so to speak, become, well, brilliant, without a doubt.'

Toby excuses himself and makes for the washroom. He is filled with anger. How could his mother keep such information from Betty and him? What a witch, a sicko. He splashes cold water on his face. 'She should be the one trying to kill herself,' he yells at the mirror. 'Fucking bitch!' He tosses more water over his face. He can see the scar, Phil's work, a jagged line etched down the side of his nose. He plays with it, runs his finger down its length, remembering the bashing, the look in Phil's eyes. More like the screen of a Lair, he thinks. No longer human.

'Hey Toby, what ya doin'? Wow, what a success. Kate must be beside herself,' Ben enthuses. 'Hey, mate, you alright?'

Toby steadies himself, pats the water that beads his face with a towel.

'Yep, yep, just a little overcome. A little out of my depth. I've never mixed with highbrows like this lot before.'

'Hah, they're certainly different. Great for Kate though,' Ben says, washing his hands. 'Come on, let's get some of those freebees into us. Can't let the bubbles go flat.'

Together they walk back into the gallery just as Warwick is tapping his glass. 'Ladies and gentlemen, and others,' he laughs. 'Thank you for attending Kate's show. It's spectacular. Vibrant. It goes without saying that Kate is one of our leading exponents of paint. I'm delighted to tell you this show is a sell-out. So you obviously agree with me when I say Kate is headed for greatness. Now, while I have your attention, I'd like to tell you that I have had the opportunity to see Kate's newest, and so far unfinished, work. A mysterious series, a collaboration, based on a novel about to be published. We hope Kate's next show will be in conjunction with the book's launch, right here at the Warwick Baship Galleries. I'd like to thank you once again for visiting the Warwick Baship Galleries. Please drink up.'

Applause erupts, drowning out Kate's words as she races towards Toby, fuming. 'Bloody little rat. Rotten bastard. Avaricious little prick!'

Toby screws up his face, his teeth pressed together.

'He saw the Superbird painting in my studio. Kinda helped himself to it. What I mean is I couldn't stop him. He's very forceful at times. Then he wanted to know where the idea came from and I told him it was inspired by your book. I said it was going to be published. I know I shouldn't have said that…' Kate is desperately searching Toby's eyes. 'Please don't hate me. I'm sorry. It's just I know it will get published. It's all in Warwick's head, the idea of doing both together. The show and the book launch. You look angry. I understand. I'm going to give him both barrels. He had no right to say such things.'

'Kate, it's okay. I don't give a toss about Warwick. It's my father. I know where he is. See that guy over there?' Toby says, pointing into the crowd. 'That tall guy with the white hair. That's our family GP. He just told me he knows where Dad lives and will give me his address.'

'That's wonderful Toby. But you don't look happy. You look upset.'

'He told me Dad tried to commit suicide, Kate.'

'Shit, Toby, how awful.'

'Dr Marsh said he's okay now, living with another woman. I think I'll go for a walk, Kate. See you at home later. Things to think about.'

'I'll come too.'

'No, no, Kate. You should stay, enjoy your time in the limelight. I'll be alright. I prefer to be alone just now.'

'Are you sure?'

'Yeah, I'm sure. Come on, I'll introduce you to Dr Marsh. He wants to meet you. He's bought a work for his clinic.' Toby leads Kate over to the doctor, does the formal introduction, then kisses Kate on the cheek and leaves the gallery.

He walks the full length of the beach, recalling the better times he had with his father. Swimming, jumping from his shoulders into the next wave racing towards them from out of the Pacific, the picnics they'd had, the feel of salt drying on his skin, then a game of cricket, a cardboard box for a wicket, a piece of wood for a bat and worn-out tennis balls the dog had chewed. He can see his father laughing at his mother with that funny run-up she always did, dancing in to chuck the ball. His father would always have to duck as it came floating in at his head. Then he'd fall to the sand, legs and arms flaying in all directions. All of them giggling.

He remembers his dad talking to the fishermen, buying a kingy straight from the boat. So chuffed he was, showing it off excitedly.

'Just look at the colour,' he said, and Betty saying, 'I don't like fish' and his dad saying, 'all the more for me then.' They were good times. Family times when the world was carefree and Toby felt he belonged. He kicks at the sand each time he thinks of his mother. How can she be so heartless, tell them Dad's gone and good riddance to bad rubbish, be so hard towards him after twenty years of marriage? She deserves Phil. The right mongrel for such a perfect bitch. How could she keep that from them? Their father tried to see them, for godsake. And he lives so near.

He sits out on the point among the boulders that balance on the slab granite shelves, snapping driftwood in his hands and casting the pieces to the sea.

This is where Kate finds him. She is still dressed in her snazzy clothes, looking like a mermaid princess, moving in and out of the cliff-face shadows, picking her way across the rocks, her heeled sandals hanging loosely from her painted nails.

She climbs up and sits next to him, puts her arm around his waist, her head against his shoulder. She says nothing, just looks out across the bay, waiting for him to talk.

'Sorry to spoil your night,' he says. 'It was such a shock to hear about Dad trying to do himself in.'

Kate, still silent, curls closer, touches his cheek.

'I don't know if I should tell Betty. She has only just stopped talking about Dad. I don't know what to do,' he says, cracking another twig. 'I hate my mum even more. The evil creep. How could she? I mean, he's our dad.'

Kate lets him spill it out. She strokes his hair.

'I feel like putting an ad in the paper, warning people about her, with a heading like "Evil Pig. Keep your children away".'

At last he is spent. They sit together, breathing quietly. He lights a smoke then throws it away.

'You should go and see him. Would you like that?'

'I'm not sure he would want it.'

'Of course he would. I'll come with you if you want.'

'I love you, Kate. I wish I hadn't found out about him tonight. You should be... we should be out celebrating your famous show.'

'We can do it at home. Got a nice bottle of red. Ben and Sharee are there. They're worried about you too.'

'I feel like some horrendous sad-sack, pulling you all down. The party pooper. I should have kept it to myself at least for tonight. I'm so sorry Kate.'

'Toby, I'm not that fazed about missing out on dinner with Warwick at some crowded place where you can't talk. I prefer being here with you. I call that success, my best work. Come on sweetie, I'm getting cold sitting here. I'm not dressed for it.'

'You look stunning. Beautiful,' he says, taking her hand to help her down from their perch and back to the sand.

Toby's Dream

Chapter Seventeen

Epic struggled, searching for the Mancirian's transmitter, gagging in the offensive air, returning again and again to breathe Oak's oxygen that she was pumping towards the Library door. Deteriorating each time he returned to explore the fire-charred scraps. He stalked the cindered bookcases, coughing, sneezing, covering his beak with his wings.

Where would the Alien have stowed it? Where would he hide such an important component. With a renewed effort, Epic flew high up towards Solo's damaged laboratory. Here the carbon was thick, lolling about the ceiling, rolling down its walls, impenetrable, the collapsed staircase hanging, dangling in mid-air. He cancelled out the lab. No one except himself could have reached such a place, especially not the massive Zebu. It was damaging being in the carbon. He fluttered erratically back down to Oak's life-giving oxygen, bracing himself against the door jamb, rocking on his tail feathers, gulping in the air.

Deeper into the corners he ventured turning burnt furniture, checking under the half-burned long table, knowing he is in trouble, that he could only last a few more minutes in this gas-chamber of toxic fumes.

He called on the Sansvira for strength, saw them in his mind fading into oblivion, vanishing into the cliff-face. He shuffled back to the doorway, bent, choking, bleary-eyed, suffocating in the deplorable blackness, afraid his sight might be going.

'Epic,' Oak's leaves chanted. 'Epic, there is a chute. A chute that leads directly to the Undercity. Find it and remove the covering that must have survived the flames. There you will find oxygen.'

Epic looked towards Oak through the pools of water that brimmed his eyes, cascading down his feathered face. The tree shimmered like some mirage in the distance. Epic steadied, drew himself up and flung his body back into the appalling void, climbing piles of brittle books that crumbled into sooty ash, half-devoured composites. Indoctrinations for the underlings that were brought above to be converted into Halflights and Lairs.

He could just make out the chute-like structure poking out from a wall several feet away. This had to be it, the thing Oak had told him of. It must be the chute. It had to be. He needed its air. But by its base were two red eyes, blinking, wavering, low to the ground watching him. Epic tried to focus, to hold on to the vision. Now, they vanished in a blur. He collapsed into the structure. The half-burnt planks still carried an acrid smell of charred wood. He ripped at them with his wings, separating the boards just enough to know he had found the precious river he so desired. Oxygen immediately penetrated the gap. He forced his beak between the cracks, prising the stubborn coverings a little wider, sucking in the wonderful scent, the gift of life. Barely conscious, spluttering, his chest heaving.

Without warning, he was grabbed from behind and slung away, smacking into the wall, crumpling, folding into himself. He had just enough wit left to meld into his surroundings and he crawled away as the two slitted, cat-like eyes came pouncing forward, searching with distraught, bony fingers, moaning. Spittle flew inches above Epic's head.

The wretched creature closed the chute, then bounced away, flinging every obstacle in its path, shattering the silence that lingered in this unholy place. Obsession blazing in its eyes, berserk, paralysing screams spilling from its twisted mouth. It too was searching, for the transmitter that Epic was risking his wings for.

Epic slid back to the chute. He pulled himself up once more and opened a crack large enough to place his beak just as Jall rushed through the Library entrance, shaking off the snow, stamping his feet, slapping his hands together, calling out Zebu's name.

Laxman ducked for cover as Jall's voice rang out, 'Zebu, Zebu, I'm here. The Kuaha are upon you. They come for your City. The light is miserable in here. I can't see. Where are you? You must protect me. Take me back to Manci with you as you promised. Show yourself.'

* * * * * * *

Zebu Manci never looked more sinister. His rage complete. Dr Steel could hear its master's heart bubbling under his fatty exterior, thermal rumblings rubbing, scrubbing some dark vital organ inside the Mancirian. Steel leaned, balancing like some topsy-turvy drunk. His Lair body, fidgety, its blades rattling and tapping a tune against each finger by its side. Its screen skipping, as if the Lair was dwelling in another world, a place of voodoo, held by an hallucinating trance, waiting to be released from its spell.

An evil odour, a reservoir of desalinating chemicals, circled around Zebu Manci's head, cranking the workings, the cogs that slipped together activating strange phone-shaped receivers that sprang in their cradles, as a sudden surge lit up his transparent bulbous head. Sharp, staccato rhythms sliced the carbon apart as Manci's tongue cracked about his ranks like a stock-whip, turning, snarling doing contortions around his mean lips.

Fifty Lairs were packed into the vault, their screens racing, testing each frequency, radiating a jumble of wild current that sizzled overhead to echo against the elevator. The square concrete cube vibrated in the dry air.

Shoving Lairs aside, Zebu strode, bristling, towards the Undercity door. He was a tempest, a tornado, bellowing 'get me fresh meat', ready to dismember as many humans as he possibly could. His clenched talons punched at the steel door, willing it to rise faster, his tongue impatiently flicking from the corner of his foaming mouth.

Dr Steel flipped back its head and howled, snapping, snipping its fingers next to its master's side. Its metal bowler hat reflected Zebu's presence like a lighthouse ablaze on a treacherous headland. There was a murderous clashing of popping screens, grunts, fingers stretching, boots clicking. A tidal wave fed through the seismic movement of Zebu's giant claws, thundering, stamping out a drumbeat as the door cleared his head. He found the Undercity gathered, waiting. Silk, at the front, standing calmly with Campbell. Neke coiled around her arm.

Zebu buckled the moment he saw her, stepped back in an involuntary jerk, swinging his talons erratically into the nearest Lair. The Lair's screen exploded. Shards flew, piercing Zebu's fatty body. He reeled away, screaming at Dr Steel to tear the woman apart.

Steel's fingers were working fiendishly as it minced forward, mystified by its master's retreat, shocked to see Campbell, backed by hundreds of weapon-wielding men advancing. Fierce battle-cries boomed from each mouth, descending without concern or fear, throwing themselves at Steel and the few jittery Lairs that had hesitantly followed it into the Undercity.

The clash was brutal. A hundred years of pent-up hatred, a swarming mass of lances, tore into Steel's body. Clubs rained against its screen; it was trampled underfoot in a violent stampede.

Zebu moaned, devastated, fleeing towards the elevator, leaving the Lairs to be annihilated, cut down by the overwhelming forces battling their way towards him. And Campbell, urging them ever forward, bayed for Zebu's death, cursing as the Mancirian, pulling at the splinters, the shrapnel that embedded his quivering fat, spat wads of phlegm into the vault as the lift's doors closed.

Zebu burst from the control room, his massive claws sinking into the snow-covered street. He passed the dormant Acheron Afrit. He raced towards the Library, heading for his only option – the transmitter he had hidden behind a panel in the gutted plug-in room where Jip had met his fate. Zebu screeched in pain, traumatised by Oak's brilliant light, festooned in flowers, as she ripped the Library steps apart with her roots.

Through the entrance he stumbled, his head rattling, conjuring extra voltage to illuminate his way.

Jall sprung from the shadows, calling out his name. 'Zebu! You're here. Your city is under attack. The Kuaha come with their trees. Call your Lairs and any who will fight for the Mancirian Empire.'

With tongue flicking, Zebu barked, 'Guard the door. I'll take you with me if you can hold them back.' Across the hall he limped, his ugly heart beating against his fat. He was close to the plug-in room, just a few strides away, when Laxman darted from it.

'Is this what you're looking for?' he snarled. He held the transmitter clutched in his bony fingers, waved it at the Mancirian's head as he leapt sideways to avoid Zebu's flaying talons.

'You will pay for your crimes,' he screamed. 'Jaars will never forget what you have done, what Mancirians are. Percolating fat, archaic, destined for extinction, toxic defilements, condemned criminals.'

The Mancirian spun, following the Jaar's leap and crying out, 'Together, we can escape this place, call for help.'

'You won't be coming with me,' Laxman snorted, dancing around the Mancirian, taunting Zebu, looking for an opening, a chance to escape.

Epic pressed the boards aside. A rush of clean air lifted him from the ground. He hovered above the jet stream, blazing a radiant blue, to speed across the Library ceiling. Then he dived, snatched the transmitter from Laxman's bony fingers, and zipped past Zebu who was caught off guard by Epic's stunning acrobatics.

The Alien, totally beside himself, screamed for Epic to give him his transmitter. Tearing at the floor with his claws, he threw whatever he could find at Epic who glided safely away, avoiding Zebu's fury.

Laxman too, sprang, leapt after Epic, but only into Zebu's deadly embrace. A mighty cracking noise of backbone being crushed, snapped, reverberated against the Library walls as Zebu, in one mad movement, tossed the broken Jaar to the floor.

Green fluid dribbled from Laxman's eyes, his mouth and parts unseen as he wriggled in his final breath, squashed under the full weight of Zebu.

* * * * * * *

Nua and I cautiously cross the massive square, expecting trouble, a few Lairs at least, still in operational order. The city's gloom is being shoved aside by the advancing cool blue of a morning sky, and the extraordinary gathering of the Truth Stream creatures, fraternising with each other, lining the outer rims of the quadrangle, as if waiting patiently for us to call them to our side.

And in the distance, Otahi and his warriors are making their way up the main avenue, darting in and out of buildings, standing over snow-covered Lairs. Turning those that need turning, systematically terminating their screens with a swing of their clubs.

Nua springs at the Library steps, taking two at a time, to shelter underneath Oak. At the tips of her branches her fragrant blossoms shimmer exquisitely against the ever-deepening azure sky.

Still apprehensive, I back my way up the broken flight of steps, eyes alert, watching for the surprise attack I am sure will still come from some fresh evil invention. But none comes.

Safely anchored against Oak's trunk, we discuss Jall's footprints that clearly lead to the Library doors. Nua exulted, impatient to extract his revenge on the head of Jall.

'You can't just go charging forward. We don't know what trap Jall might have devised or if he is still alone. It will be pitch-black inside the home of the Mancirian, who can light its own way,' I say.

I rub on Oak's trunk. My fingers feel warm on her bark.

'Place your hands on Oak, Nua,' I say. 'You have forgotten to pay your respects to the mighty tree, so bound up have we been in tracking Jall.

Look at her. How magnificent she stands, cleansing the air. Jall could not get to within twenty paces of her. She would have swiped him from the earth. We know he's treacherous and cunning. We would be wise to wait, to ask Oak for counsel.'

Nua is about to remind me that Oak didn't detect Jall's traitor heart, that Jall had fooled her, but he bites his lip and places one hand on Oak while squeezing his club in the other.

'Lay down your weapon for just one moment, Nua,' Oak's leaves whisper overhead. 'Feel my own growing pains. Try to understand I am fallible. Just like you. I had to make judgements I thought were right. Jall was planted so carefully by Zekai. I missed it. His master was crafty clever. I too, want his life force near my branches so I may strangle him and cast him down these steps. Jall's betrayal has haunted me. I've seen him in this city many times talking to Zebu. Imagine how it tortured me, being hacked into the Mancirian's likeness, knowing I could not let your people know of Jall's betrayal. I tried; my only option was to relay it to the woman Silk, to Epic, so he could catch the devil at his handiwork. That's how the Superbird finally discovered him attacking my acorns after stealing them from Solo's basket.'

Nua lets his club drop. It dangles from his wrist. He now places both hands on Oak, feels the strength, the pulse of the tree vibrating down his arms, ashamed at himself for his negative thoughts.

'Oak,' he replies. 'It's been such a strain living in the woods alone, questioning my own sanity. At times I lost all love. I feel yours now filling my heart, returning it to how it should be, strong and true. I understand the futility of hate and how it eats at one's soul, turns it to dust to blow away. I no longer have room for hate.

'I will kill Jall with love, with love in my club, for I do it for the Truth Stream, to purge it of an evil life-form. Not for personal revenge, but a higher cause. I will take your limbs and trunk with me as I strike.'

I watch, delighted to see Nua's face relax. His tattoos return to their flowing lines, a sparkle to his eyes – no longer the dead black eyes of night that had lost their way. The transformation is like one of Oak's flowers, opening to celebrate the return of the sun.

'Jall is sneaky and crude. He is panicking behind the Library door, waiting for you or any that come, doing his master's bidding,' Oak says, rubbing her branches together. 'And Zebu and the Jaar Laxman squabble over who will rule Lair City. Epic of the Superbirds also does battle inside while we talk.'

'I have a plan. I will draw him out,' I say. 'Then I'll step aside. You, Nua, can do the deed that we all long for. Jall's head will fall.'

I stand, calling out his name at the Library's entrance. 'Jall, it's Solo,' I scream. No reply comes. 'What? Scared of me, you gutless dog? You're a freak of nature, you're not wanted in this land or any other. You must die, Jall.'

I hear a scraping sound like a piece of wood being raised from the floor. Then Jall springs out in full sight, ready to beat in my skull.

'You're the freak, Solo, not me, I'll enjoy putting you in the ground,' he screams as the length of timber he wields starts to rip through the air.

Suddenly, Nua is there, reaching out for Jall's arm, snapping his club high over his head with his other, bringing it down, with a mighty crack, in one fluid motion.

Jall goes to open his mouth, while dropping the timber from his limp hand. Quizzically, his eyes flick in his head, and somehow he nods once in recognition of Nua's tight clenched teeth and smiling lips that say, 'No, Jall, you're the freak.'

Nua casually spins him around, places his foot on Jall's back and laughs, pushing him through the door.

Jall slumps, tottering back into the Library. His hands press to both sides of his head as he staggers towards Zebu. Blood trickles between his trembling fingers, as he makes his way from the entrance and the silhouetted, befeathered figure of Nua holding a club above his head. Jall raises his hands, pleading to Zebu for help, exposing a shattered hole from which his brain seeps. He collapses face-down. His head splits like a melon on the Library floor.

Nua moves forward through the entrance. I roar like a lion for him to stop, to keep well away from the Alien, pulling him back to the door frame.

'That hideous creature can spit a corrosive chemical that will eat through your body. Just wait. We have it cornered. Superbird nearly died from its toxic phlegm, remember?'

Epic arrives, glides over and places the transmitter in my hand. 'Solo is right, Nua. We have to be very careful. Keep a safe distance.'

Zebu sneaks closer, head blazing, sucking deeply on his tubes. 'Give me the transmitter and I will leave your planet. It's a world that holds no interest for me or Manciria. The air is foul. Unbreathable, poisonous to our kind. Your trees and grass inflict pain on our sensitive bodies.

I have to contact Manci, report on what I have found. You have my word your planet is unsuitable for our expansionist plans. I realise this now. Seeing Zekai fail should have been a warning. I wanted to leave then, but the Jaar demanded we stay. I have finished its life. It's broken inside, deeper in. Come, have a look. You can do what you want with it. A gift from me to you. Just give me the transmitter and I'll be on my way. Come on, come closer, have a look at it. Trust me. I have done work for you. Delivered an enemy. Come, see. I only want that component. It means nothing to you.'

'Then come and get it,' I say, holding it up to the Alien while stepping back out of the Library door into the portico.

Zebu stalks forward, tracking us. We are leading the Alien into the streets of Lair city. With each step, the Alien's deplorable condition becomes more exposed. It cringes in the sunlight, wrapping its arms around its head, its body seeping a dark ooze. Its tongue slaps against its side as it whimpers, pleading for the transmitter.

The quadrangle, sparkling under an impossibly perfect sky, is blanketed with snow. Otahi and his warriors stand stunned by the sight of the monstrous creature awkwardly making its way down the shattered Library steps.

'Don't touch it. Keep well away,' I yell.

Now we have Zebu. It prowls, making a noise like a crying kitten, gnashing its teeth. Its talons are held out, gesturing pitifully towards me. Gunk drips from its mouth, sizzling as it hits the snow, melting a path in front of it. Then it squeals – a high-pitched noise – and grabs at its globules as Silk appears from behind my shoulder, radiant, glowing. Her hooded cape, caressing her face, falls to cover her feet. It seems as if she is gliding forward above the snow towards the Alien, stopping only inches from its cringing body. Quietly, she tells it, 'Zebu Manci, you are now alone.'

It bends its head to the ground and its talons twist, forming a fist. The creatures from the Truth Stream now venture forward, peering between the legs of the gathered, here to witness the victory of the Truth Stream.

Silk moves to pick up a white rabbit that has hopped to her side. She holds it, cradles it in her arms, stroking the rabbit's head. Campbell's heart jumps in his chest, frightening a fox by his feet. I call to him to stand his ground.

The quadrangle is brimming with the Undercity dwellers, delivered at last from their underground hell. All are fascinated by Silk's amazing courage, intoning her name, not knowing if they should celebrate their freedom or attack en masse one last time. Campbell, biting his nails, anxiously looks to me then back at Silk. I move my head in response and form the word 'no' with my lips. He blinks, then swallows hard.

Zebu groans and steps away. Steam drifts from under his clawed feet. Silk herds the Alien to where she knows he belongs. Zebu backs away until she has him in Data Street and in the shadow of Acheron Afrit, under its thorny branches, howling, doubled in pain.

'You know this tree,' she says, 'and it knows you. It has bodies of my people under its roots but no longer grows. It has shut down because you fed Jaars to its blind mouth. And though it can't see, it can taste the flesh and knows what it devours. It waits for only one to pass its way, and that is you. It has a memory, and belongs with the Jaars on their planet, not here. It knows you're standing defeated. It can smell you and wants nothing more than your foul, fatty soul. Repayment for your blasphemy, your cold worthless life. Look at me. Lift your head. See us all here? Every creature every, human. We belong to, and cherish, this world.'

Zebu shakes. He lifts his bulbous, transparent head, now as black as the rest of his shrinking body, collapsing into itself, pawing at the snow with a weak, clawed foot.

Acheron Afrit snaps into life. Its limbs swing wildly, whistling through the air, its trunk as black as Zebu's fat. Expanding, as if taking a breath, then shuddering violently, ripping a lower bough from its side. It quivers, its sharpened thorns crawling with ticks. Then it arches itself and strikes, impaling Zebu right through his abdomen, lifting him to the opening of the crater at its base, plunging the Alien into its dark recess, deep underground.

The crowd, hushed, chilled by the spectacle, look to each other, aware that this is the hated flesh-eating tree. They wait for Silk to back away, anxious that she might be next to feed its sick life force.

'Silk,' they plead as one. She does not turn or acknowledge their concern. She strokes the rabbit, talks to it, and then puts it down in the snow. It hops around the tree. Three times it circles, then returns to her, stands at her feet while the topmost branches wreathe, start to wilt, shrivel down their length in a chain reaction. Its trunk blistering, smoke curling from its bark, the tree ignites. The flames spring from limb to limb until a blazing inferno is reflected in the snow.

The city erupts into cheers. People dance around each other, throw down their weapons to embrace the nearest. They are delirious with relief, smiling, laughing, leaping up and down, at last taking in the glorious sun, the beautiful sky, and the clean air, adorned with flowers dropping miraculously from the heavens.

* * * * * * *

Silk walks among them, accepting their joyous thanks. Campbell races to her side. 'Where are Epic and Solo?' she asks him, 'and the mystical one Neke?' Campbell says he does not know.

'Then come with me,' she says with a twinkle in her eye. 'I know where they will be.'

'Silk, you're an angel that none dares hurt or speak ill of. It's your pure heart, your knowledge, your love that streams before you, that embraces your every part. How conceited of me to think I could protect that which does not need protection. How right you were when you said there is only love.'

'Campbell, now that the Truth Stream has been released, we can live in this way. I remember I once told you that perhaps we could walk together some day. I'm ready to keep your company now. I too, have been freed. My vigilance is finished.

'Like other women I have the urge to make a home, to care for a family. I'm no different. Here, take my hand. I do need protection, dear man, a place to dwell, some happy times in the Truth Stream. Look, see, there they are,' she says, leading Campbell into the massive square.

Neke coos in Oak's branches, Epic by her side, and Powerflower hovers close by. Solo is in one branch, arm around Nua's shoulders, their legs dangling, laughing, calling to Keywee who struts around the tree trumpeting sweet sounds to the gathered Kuaha, as Otahi calls to his brother.

'Come down. We all can't fit in the tree. I have a gift. Please Nua.'

'Go dear friend, your Chief needs you. Let's see what he has, that he is so keen to give.'

Nua jumps down from the tree, and Chief Otahi removes his cloak of the finest feathers and places it over Nua. The Kuaha all chant Nua's name. A tear runs down his proud face. Applause breaks out in the quadrangle. Humans from the Undercity, and all creatures great and small from the Truth Stream, are singing, calling, barking, as one voice.

Campbell's face brims over with love, and he leans into Silk. She places a kiss on his lips.

'Oak, I must go to release the Sansvira from their imprisonment. The Superbirds will live again in the realm of Man. We will multiply,' Epic says.

'Don't leave in such a hurry, Epic. This day has just begun. Look my friend, straight ahead. I think you might just fall from my tree.'

Epic straightens, stares from Oak's blossoming branches and then leaps into the sky as five Superbirds in formation ply the heavens. One has the Ahorangi balanced on its back, and the other four are carrying Bella, Race, Count Keith and Angel Cupcake. They land beside the swaying tree as Race cries out, 'By jingoes, Bella, look, it's Solo.'

Chapter Eighteen

It's a cloudless day, hot and bright. The cottage, surrounded by flowers, a bonanza of colour kept in check by a white picket fence, is three streets back from the beach. They sit in Kate's brand new VW, a reward for all her work. Toby squirms in the passenger seat, staring out across the road at the blue front door.

'You ready for this?' she asks.

'Don't know, now that I'm here. What do I say? Dr Marsh told me you tried to kill yourself, I'm here to tell you not to be so stupid?'

'Toby, just tell him that you found out where he lives and you just want to let him know that you're thinking of him, would he like to come for dinner at our place? Like we worked out on the way over here. There will be time later to talk about other things.'

'Yeah, like, hey Dad, why'd ya try to cut ya throat?'

'Toby, come on, don't worry your pretty head with words you know you won't say. Take a deep breath. Come on, let's go.

'It's a gorgeous little house,' Kate says as Toby swings the gate back on itself.

There are bumble bees milking pollen, a butterfly slips past, sliding in freefall, then works its iridescent wings in a fit of energy to disappear around the corner of the house. Toby's hands are sweaty. He rubs them against his jeans and knocks on the door, stepping back to stand with his arm around Kate, nervously looking at his feet.

'There's no one here,' he says, after a few seconds. 'It's a mistake. Let's go.'

'Knock again,' Kate says. 'He might not have heard. Go on, Toby, knock.'

He is half way up the doorstep when a woman comes around the side of the building, looking as colourful as the butterfly that has just floated by. She has a large straw sunhat sending a shadow across her pleasant face, a trowel in one of her dirt-stained gloves and a seedling in the other.

'Yes, can I help you?' she asks. Then, coming closer, manoeuvring herself past the flowerbeds to peer at Toby, 'You're Toby,' she says. 'This is a lovely surprise. Your father will be thrilled. He's around the back.' She places her gardening tool and seedling down, removes her gloves and offers her hand in greeting.

'I'm Gwen,' she says.

Toby turns to Kate. 'This is Kate.'

'Nice to meet you Kate,' Gwen says, smiling, leading them in the direction from which she'd come.

His dad is turning soil in a vegie plot, humming to himself.

'Christopher, you have visitors,' Gwen says brightly. He looks up from his work to see the three of them grouped together, all smiles.

'I'll make some tea,' Gwen offers, and steps into the house.

'Toby, son. Oh, it's so good to see you,' Christopher says, brushing the soil from his hands, jumping out of the garden to race to Toby's side and hug him.

Gwen has removed her hat and is watching from the kitchen window, tears rolling down her cheeks.

'This is Kate, Dad.'

He swivels, grinning and says, 'So, so glad you are here, Kate.'

'I'll go and help Gwen,' she says, leaving the two of them to get reacquainted, to savour the moment together.

* * * * * * *

'That was awesome,' Toby enthuses while driving back to their place. 'He looks so well, so happy. Gwen seems such a nice woman, so caring and gentle, fully at home.'

'He loves you, Toby. You see? How about all those photos of Betty and you lining the mantelpiece and side table. I'm so happy for you and your dad. Thrilled to be part of such a magic day.'

'Man, it blew me out when he said he knew your work, had read the review of your last show. Didn't think he cared for art or creative pursuits. He even knew your last name.'

'He was over the moon about your writing, over the moon to hear that Betty was doing so well at school. Gwen's a darling. I don't think you have to worry about your dad any more.'

* * * * * * *

'It's for you, Toby,' Ben yells. 'The phone. Someone wants you.'

'Hi. Toby Miller. What? Yes. Today. Two o'clock. Okay. Yes, alright.' Toby stands with the receiver in his hand, then screams 'Yahoo! Wow!'

'What's happening,' Ben says. 'You won Lotto or something?'

'That was Earth Publications. Gerald. They want to publish my book.'

'Bloody hell, you're kidding me,' Ben cries, calling through the house. 'Sharee, Sharee, Earth Publications's going to publish Toby's book.'

Kate comes running from her room, Sharee from the kitchen, all at once, jumping up and down, grabbing Toby, shaking him, slapping high fives.

Toby scratches at his head. 'How did they get hold of the draft manuscript? I didn't give it to them.'

'I did. I gave it to Gerald. So much has been going on, I forgot to tell you Toby. I'm sorry, I hope it's okay,' Kate says sheepishly.

'It's outrageous. Far out, babe.' And he grabs her, kisses her a dozen times while dancing on the spot.

* * * * * * *

Summer hit its straps, long evenings, barbeques, swimming, pool parties with live bands. For the first few weeks, Sharee and Ben say, 'Come on, let's go down and look at Toby's book and window display,' and they stand on the pavement outside the bookstore and say, 'We know that guy.'

Toby says silly things like, 'Love to meet him, can you make it happen for me?' And he spins on the spot waving his arms in the air.

They make him read every word of the trilogy to them, grossing out at the horror of the Mancirians, Marvin Shanks, Smelt and the Lairs, and cheering when Solo escapes, taking Bella and Race.

Then a letter arrives with invitations from Toby's publisher, stating that his book has made the final selection for the *The Lim Awards*. That he must attend in formal attire. That it's important he be there.

Kate leads him to a suit hire outfitter. 'For the best dressed', the sign confirms. They dress him from top to toe. 'You could get the part of 007,' she squeals. 'Shaken, not stirred.'

It's a line the store-keeper must have heard a thousand times over. With his tape draped around his shoulders and rolling his eyes with an 'oh-not-that-again' look, he says, 'You look splendid Mr Miller; have the suit back by ten o'clock, will you please.'

* * * * * * *

In the hotel foyer, the crowds mill. It is a calendar highlight, a dazzling event that surpasses even one of Kate's glamorous openings. For the invited only. Industry people, writers and their partners, gossip columnists, reviewers, the Prime Minister, celebrities with well-known faces, and patrons of the arts. Gerald, waiting with his PA, broadly smiling, bathes in the spotlight. He kisses Kate, then shepherds them to their table close to the stage, acknowledging greetings, a wave here, a nod there.

'I have a good feeling about this, Toby. I think we have a winner. Your book's super. Just the right tone for our modern age – an environmental fantasy, a grand tale. As far as I can tell, you only have one serious contender in your category, Lewis Smith's *A Place Too Far*. I'm a little jittery. You know it will send your sales through the roof if you win this award.'

Kate places her hand on Toby's knees, which are clicking together under the table. He fidgets with his napkin and looks around the room, hardly touching his wine.

'Did you write something like I asked?' Gerald enquires, somewhat seriously, across the table. 'If not, Shirley's jotted a few lines for you, just in case.' He passes Shirley's notes towards Toby, who waves them away.

'No, I'll be alright. But I'm a bit scared you might have built up your hopes. What if I come last?'

'Don't you believe that for one second. My ferrets have had their noses to the ground. The word is that it's a close thing between you and Lewis. That's him over there. The guy with his hair slicked down, next to that awful woman with the purple hair and tattoos climbing out of her breasts. Wanted to bring her dog in earlier. Thank God it was turned away. A little weasel-looking thing, all teeth with a giant bow like some packaged gift you'd give to Frankenstein's monster. Well, here we go. It's your category next.'

Kate squeezes Toby's hand.

A luscious, well-known blonde TV hostess fiddles with the envelope and passes it to Johnston Sharpe of multi-media fame.

'I can't look,' the blonde says, as he turns it her way. The room, totally silent, waits for her to say, 'And the winner is…Toby Miller for *The Birth of Superbird*.'

Gerald jumps out of his seat, flies around the table, slapping Toby on his back, clapping madly, stepping back a pace to allow him out of his chair.

Toby leans, kisses Kate, winks and strolls up the steps, accepting the hand of Johnston Sharpe and a peck from the blonde, both applauding, moving out of the way of the rostrum for Toby to address the crowd.

'For the longest winter, I thought I was trapped in a world lost to mayhem, tragedy, cruelty, one totally absorbed in winning at any cost to the earth. The struggle I was having with this I internalised, turned into the fantasy world of Lair City and the underworld of the corrupt and evil Aliens. My sources were TV docos, newsreels and the printed page. The hard facts that we are bombarded with each day – of war, pestilence, bird flu, GE, test-tube babies, carbon footprints, ecological disasters, famine and violence.

'I packaged, wrapped up, my story inside these events and only just managed to box my way out of hopelessness into the light of day with imagined creatures and people like Solo, Bella and Race. Through them I found I could believe in something close to love – the central theme of Silk and Oak and the Ahorangi of the Kuaha. I now realise there's so much more to the world than the destitute and creepy underbelly I dwelled in for those three years.

'I'm thrilled you like my book and advise you to mix your reading with stories that brighten up your lives, those filled with compassion, those that are full of love. I see my book as an entertainment, nothing more.

'Before I finish, I have to say I owe the biggest thanks to Kate Carlton, Ben Lock and Sharee Bartlett for helping me find my way, encouraging me to finish *The Birth of Superbird*. For, if I hadn't met such a fine collection of friends, I don't believe the book would ever have been finished.

'I must not forget to thank Gerald Gould of Earth Publications, who also believed in the book enough to put it forward for this prize.'

Toby makes his way back to his table, the spotlight tracking him all the way, till he sits, placing his trophy on the table next to Gerald.

* * * * * * *

'Shall we walk home through the park?' he asks Kate.

'Of course,' she says. 'Whatever you want, my darling author.'

Out on the street, he is taken aback at the sight of Betty waiting with their mum, off to one side. Betty skips across.

'Hey, we heard you won. That's amazing, Toby. My brother's a star.'

Toby tries hard to show his sister his joy, but glares across at his mother where she hovers in the shadows, her two hands clutching one another.

'Mum's left Phil. Had him carted away by the cops. Been three weeks now. She stopped drinking, took me to see Dad yesterday. She's so, so, sorry for what she has done to us. She needs our help, Toby. Please give her that chance. Please.'

He looks at Kate, who smiles and places a hand on his back. 'Go on, Toby, remember what you just told your fans.'

Betty stands on his shoe and says, 'Toby, she's our mum.'

Together they go across to meet her as she inches her way towards them, clearly emotional, not knowing how to behave in his company.

'Betty tells me you've stopped drinking, got rid of Phil the garbage man.' Kate arrives at his side. 'This is Kate.'

'Hello Mrs Miller,' Kate says, extending her hand.

'Hear you took Betty to see Dad. And Gwen,' he adds, so she is not mistaken about his dad being happy now.

His mother's face quivers slightly as she fights back her tears. Kate has her arms draped down Betty's front as she stands behind her, wanting Toby to let go of all his anger, embrace his mum, and tell her that he really loves her. But she knows it will take time for his wounds to heal.

'Good to see you, Mum. I'll come around soon. Just give me a day or two.'

His mother gives a relieved little smile and says, 'I love you son.'

'That's great,' Toby replies. 'See you Betty,' he says brightly. 'In a day or two.'

'Okay, Toby. You will come, won't you?'

'Sure, Betty. I'll be there. Ring you to let you know.'

Kate and Toby stroll away with Kate looking back over her shoulder. She gives a tiny wave to Betty and his mum. She can hear Betty saying excitedly, 'See, I told you, Mum.'

They walk and talk, sit in the park, get up and walk some more. Arm-in-arm with a swagger, and laughing, kissing, then letting out a 'whoopee' from time to time, and then sit again on a wooden bench near a large old pohutukawa tree. Its branches, partly lit from the side, finger the night overhead .

There are flashes of blue that dive through the boughs before coming to rest in full sight. A pair of black tail feathers caught in elegant triangles, and egg-shaped white breasts. Their eyes flash open, shut, and then they fly away.

Toby and Kate look at each other, speechless. They spring to their feet to try and follow, but the birds have disappeared. Now, down the path, out of the darkness comes a Kuaha-looking chap with a moko, a full-face tattoo. He stops and asks, 'You haven't seen a pair of blue birds about this big?' He demonstrates their size with his hands.

'Friends of yours?' Toby asks.

'Yes, you could say that.'

Kate jumps up and plants a kiss on the man's face, and then turns and points to the sky.

They see tail feathers sticking out from his plaited hair as he gazes, following her point of reference to some place in the heavens, and he says, 'Ah, the Truth Stream.'

New Beginnings